KT-448-581

THE HUNT FOR IRON EYES

Iron Eyes is pursuing ruthless outlaws Joe Hyams and Buster Jones.
But the pair get the drop on him, and
leave him for dead in the dust . . .
Meanwhile, another man is on the
bounty hunter's trail — gunfighter
Wolfe, sworn to take his revenge on
the man who left him missing one
arm. Kidnapping Squirrel Sally, the
woman besotted with Iron Eyes, Wolfe
sets off across the prairie — intending to use her as bait to draw out his
enemy . . .

Books by Rory Black
in the Linford Western Library:

THE FURY OF IRON EYES
THE WRATH OF IRON EYES
THE CURSE OF IRON EYES
THE SPIRIT OF IRON EYES
THE GHOST OF IRON EYES
IRON EYES MUST DIE
THE BLOOD OF IRON EYES
THE REVENGE OF IRON EYES
IRON EYES MAKES WAR
IRON EYES IS DEAD
THE SKULL OF IRON EYES
THE SHADOW OF IRON EYES
THE VENOM OF IRON EYES
IRON EYES THE FEARLESS
THE SCARS OF IRON EYES
A ROPE FOR IRON EYES

RORY BLACK

THE
HUNT FOR
IRON EYES

Complete and Unabridged

LINFORD
Leicester

First published in Great Britain in 2014 by
Robert Hale Limited
London

First Linford Edition
published 2016
by arrangement with
Robert Hale Limited
London

Copyright © 2014 by Rory Black
All rights reserved

A catalogue record for this book is available
from the British Library.

ISBN 978–1–4448–2786–6

HEREFORDSHIRE
LIBRARIES

Published by
F. A. Thorpe (Publishing)
Anstey, Leicestershire

Set by Words & Graphics Ltd.
Anstey, Leicestershire
Printed and bound in Great Britain by
T. J. International Ltd., Padstow, Cornwall

This book is printed on acid-free paper

Dedicated to Eileen Gunn

Prologue

Death has an aroma like no other. It fills flared nostrils and turns even the strongest of guts. Yet to some that sickening stench meant nothing. Even when mixed with the choking smoke of discharging weapons it simply told the ruthless that their very own lives were balanced on the precipice.

It was kill or die. There was no third option. When the shooting started a certain breed of men knew they had to respond quickly or end up dead. Who or whatever started the slaughter was unimportant to those who had the smell of death already embedded in their corrupted souls. They instinctively reacted with their six-shooters and killed anyone within spitting distance.

Most of those who rode the untamed West knew that there was no place for sentiment in a world ruled by gun law.

No time to hesitate if you wanted to see another sunset.

They had to kill or end up on Boot Hill buried in a shallow grave. It was a choice even those with the lamest of brains could calculate. There was only one rule and that was to remain alive whilst others died. If the Grim Reaper wanted their heartless souls he had to work hard in order to capture them. There were books filled with the laws of the land but all had been written by pompous men who lived far away in fine granite houses. None of them knew the reality which their great country's expansion had created. Throughout the ages all laws had been made by those far more affluent than the majority.

None of them had any experience of what it was like across the famed Pecos. Life was cheap beyond civilization. In the West horses had more value than men, women or even children.

These were brutal times for pitiless souls.

The good and the bad played by the

same hymn book. It became difficult to tell the difference between those who were on one side of the law and those who were on the other. Apart from those who wore tin stars it was often impossible to distinguish who was killing whom. And only a fool would even try.

The most despised of all who dished out lethal venom with their weaponry were the unregulated bounty hunters, for they rode a line that skimmed the border between right and wrong and defied anyone to point out the difference. Some crossed that line willingly whilst others tried to remain on the right side of the law, but even the most righteous could be tempted when hunger or desperation sank its fangs into their innards.

There was no black or white in the West, only infinite shades of grey. Right and wrong might have been clearly defined in leather-bound law books, but when faced with blazing guns and trying to survive not even the most honest of men had time to read.

Yet among all who died violently in the West, most who fell victim to the merciless bullets were law-abiding people. It was real easy to get killed when gun hammers were mindlessly fanned without thought for those in the line of fire.

Sadly, the innocent discovered that grim fact all too often. These were people who simply did not manage to notice when the ruthless or the insane were about to open up with their lethal hardware.

Those who lived by their skill with their chosen weapons lived a little longer than most in the untamed landscape of the West, but it was not just the speed at drawing and firing a gun that allowed them to survive a brutal shoot-out: it was also the ability to duck fast when the bullets started to fly.

The scent of death lingered in every town throughout the emerging West. It lingered on from what had already occurred and foretold what was about to happen.

Death did indeed have a smell.

A few men carried that sickening stench with them wherever they ventured. It was a constant reminder of all their previous slayings. Just as with those who toil in slaughterhouses for a living, the smell of blood clings to every sinew of a killer's being.

No amount of carbolic soap could ever wash it away. It oozed from each pore of their heartless beings and dripped like the blood of their countless victims.

Most of the men who lived by their prowess with guns were wanted dead or alive for their devilish crimes. Most, but not all.

A few were those who hunted the wanted outlaws.

They were barely on the right side of the law themselves but they lived by the same unwritten code. They killed before they themselves were gunned down. Most followed the rules whilst a handful simply did what they had to do in order to get the job done.

Of all of the bounty hunters who roamed the West in search of those the law had failed to find, one man stood apart from the rest of his profession. He was the most feared of them all and every outlaw knew that when he had your Wanted poster in his pocket, he would never quit until he had claimed his reward money.

His name was Iron Eyes.

Some said he was a living ghost.

A few believed he was Satan himself.

Others considered him to be little more than a bloodthirsty creature trying to die but always failing. He was a misfit, a man whose name alone was feared and despised in equal portion by white men and Indians alike. Whatever he truly was he was unlike any other.

When he rode his magnificent palomino stallion his long mane of black hair moved on his broad shoulders like the wings of a giant black bat.

This was not a man like other men. This was a monstrous creature who wore evidence of every fight and battle he had ever been involved in upon his scarred face and body. If death itself had a face it was his.

It was said that Iron Eyes could not die because he was already dead but neither Heaven nor Hell wanted his emaciated carcass. Others believed that he had made a pact with the Devil and was invulnerable. The hideous scars that twisted the flesh on his face and thin, skeletal body disproved and made a mockery of that theory.

It seemed impossible that any one man could have been maimed so badly and still remain alive, yet the haunting figure still rode his powerful mount in pursuit of those with bounty on their heads.

Whatever the infamous Iron Eyes truly was, he was good at his job. There was no better hunter of men. There were few who could match his prowess with his Navy Colts for either speed or accuracy.

Yet even the most horrific of creatures had a weakness.

The infamous hunter of wanted men was no exception.

Iron Eyes did not even know it but he had a heart. It might have been blackened over the years as he plied his unholy trade but it was there all the same.

Even though he mercilessly killed those who were wanted dead or alive for the bounty money on their heads, Iron Eyes had never been able to turn his emaciated back on anyone who required his help.

The old, the weak and the poor had all at some time begged for his help and he had always willingly obliged. Not once had he ever sought praise or payment for risking his hide to help those who could not defend themselves.

It was a trait which had cost him dearly over the years but even someone whom most considered to be nothing more than a monster had his Achilles heel.

Buried deep inside his thin body there was a spark of humanity still flickering. The bounty hunter had realized long before that he had nowhere to go where people would welcome him. All he knew was how to hunt and how to kill his chosen prey.

The lean horseman fearlessly whipped and spurred the high-shouldered palomino stallion ever onward towards his eventual destiny.

Death rode on his shoulder as it had always done.

It rode with Iron Eyes.

1

Iron Eyes lashed his long leathers from side to side over the head of the mighty palomino stallion and urged it on. They cracked like a whip in the near-silent prairie. A huge black cloud covered the moon far above the horseman as the infamous bounty hunter drove his mount down through the soft sand of a ridge and back on to the stagecoach trail that linked the remote settlements along the endless border.

The hoofs of the muscular stallion thundered on the ground as it maintained its breakneck gallop. A plume of dust curled heavenwards from the hoofs of the mighty horse as its master rose up from his saddle and balanced in his stirrups. Iron Eyes knew that he had made the right decision in choosing to cut across the arid terrain in order to gain ground on the two outlaws he was hunting.

Hills and gulches were no problem for a stallion such as the one the bounty hunter rode. Iron Eyes had reduced the distance between himself and his prey by almost half. The palomino stallion had not even broken sweat as its master steered it down through a dried ravine and back up to where the starlit sand was flat and barren. The determined rider screwed up his eyes and looked ahead at a strange dark patch of vegetation. He knew that it was a perfect place from which anyone with a rifle might ambush an approaching horseman, but Iron Eyes did not slow his pace.

He just kept staring ahead as though daring anyone with the skill or guts to pick him off to try their luck. Iron Eyes sat firm in his saddle and rammed his vicious spurs into the flesh of the galloping animal beneath him.

The dark vegetation became more impressive the closer the rider rode towards it. It was a forest of Joshua trees and high cactus. It stretched across the trail five miles from the town of Twin Forks. A crude road had been carved through them a few years earlier but it still remained a perfect place for the unwary traveller to be bush-whacked, and in its time had seen more than a dozen such atrocities. It was said that the sand along the trail was stained with the blood of more than a hundred men, but that did not frighten the likes of Iron Eyes. He spurred even harder.

Iron Eyes knew that at any moment the shooting might start yet he pressed on. If they did start shooting, he told himself, they had better not miss or he would ride his horse straight down their throats.

He knew they were close. So close that he imagined he could actually smell them. The intrepid bounty hunter had two fresh Wanted posters in his deep trail-coat pockets and he was determined to lay claim to the reward money on both the outlaws' heads. Ever since he had decided to turn his hunting prowess from animals to the far more profitable outlaws, Iron Eyes had never shied away from danger.

Unlike so many other men in his unholy profession, Iron Eyes never quit.

It was only over when his prey was dead.

The sky above the prairie was black and filled with a million stars as Iron Eyes continued his approach at full gallop towards the outcrop of strange Joshua trees. To anyone who had never seen the weird trees before it might have seemed as though a number of hideous giants were gathered in a phalanx before him. Their branches were like arms covered in porcupine quills. They stretched in all directions from the twisted trunks, ready to tear the flesh from anything that got too close. The bounty hunter had ridden this way many times before in pursuit of wanted men.

It was not the trees or the towering cactus that troubled Iron Eyes but the men who might be secreted amid them. Then brief shafts of light filtered down from the sky as the black cloud gradually began to move away from the moon.

The smooth stretch of sand between the thundering palomino and the dense forest of prairie trees began to show patches of bright, eerie light. They moved as the cloud got thinner above the horse and its master. The stallion sensed danger and started to snort.

Iron Eyes knew never to ignore the honed senses of his magnificent mount. It might have just been the way the light was shifting over the sand that was troubling the palomino, he reasoned. But it might have been that his horse had seen something ahead of them that Iron Eyes himself had yet to spot.

He gripped his reins tightly in his bony left hand, leaned back and slowed his palomino stallion. Iron Eyes knew that the dark trees were still beyond the range of his prized Navy Colts, but he was well within the range of a repeating rifle.

The horse continued to snort.

Something was wrong. Iron Eyes looked all around him at the sand. It was a featureless expanse that provided nowhere for a man to take cover.

For the first time since he had set out after the two outlaws Iron Eyes felt vulnerable. Had he ridden into a trap? Had he allowed his own craving for killing to get the better of him?

His mind raced.

For days he had been hunting two ruthless outlaws named Joe Hyams and Buster Jones. Iron Eyes had learned that they had been spotted heading towards the distant settlement of Twin Forks and as they were worth over $1,000 each, the infamous bounty hunter had decided that he wanted that blood money.

What Iron Eyes had not realized was that both outlaws had spotted him following them.

Deep in the forest, with its vicious undergrowth, the outlaws lay in wait. They had known since sunup that someone was trailing them. This was not a terrain to allow the hunter to use cover to conceal his determined chase. Throughout the day Hyams and Jones had watched the rider as he had followed their trail through the desolate prairie. Even when he had taken a short cut and crossed the hills they had not lost sight of him for more than a few heartbeats.

When nightfall came they had decided to end their pursuer's chase and his life for good. Both of the outlaws were known for their ability with their Winchesters, and as they saw the distinctive palomino riding through the starlight towards them they cocked their weapons and took aim.

Few ever managed to get the drop on Iron Eyes.

None had ever succeeded in getting close to killing him.

There were few sights as terrifying as that of the infamous bounty hunter in full cry. Both outlaws looked down the barrels of their rifles and stroked their triggers as Iron Eyes rode closer and

17

closer. The tall stallion was again spurred and advanced towards their hiding-place. Both Hyams and Jones trained their Winchesters upon him.

The eerie moonlight flickered across the sand between the outlaws and the rider. It taunted their eyes and made it impossible to aim their carbines with any degree of certainty.

Then suddenly the bright moon broke completely free of the dark cloud. Its light beamed down on to the horseman and illuminated his every hideous feature. His mane of long, black, matted hair moved like the wings of some unearthly creature upon his broad shoulders. With each stride of the huge stallion Iron Eyes closed the distance between them. It was like looking at the Devil.

'That's sure one ugly varmint,' Hyams said.

'Do you know who that is, Joe?' Jones gulped as beads of sweat trailed down from his hair.

'I got me a feeling I do, Buster.'

'That's Iron Eyes.' Jones inhaled deeply. 'There can't be two men that look like that.'

'Yep, I reckon you might be right.'

Both men steadied their nerves as best they could and then looked through their rifle sights. For what seemed an eternity they simply watched the horseman thundering towards the forest of jagged thorns. Then each squeezed his trigger at almost the same moment.

Two vicious tapers of red-hot fury exploded from their rifle barrels and carved trails through the moonlight. With the deafening sound of their shots still echoing in their ears the two outlaws rose up from the sand and watched their handiwork.

Iron Eyes had seen the smoke encircle the rifle barrels but it had been too late. He had no time to do anything but wait.

Wait for the bullets to arrive.

Blood splattered up into the moonlight above the head of the horseman. It

19

sparkled in the air like a myriad precious gems. The impact rocked the bounty hunter like a blow from a clenched fist. One bullet had continued on its way but the other had found its target. It had glanced across the right side of his temple and then lifted his long black hair as it ripped a path through flesh right down to the bone.

His hands released their grip on his reins. He was lifted upward by the sheer force of the bullet.

He felt as though he had ridden into a solid wall. As if his head was being torn from his scrawny neck. Iron Eyes went cartwheeling over the cantle of his ornate saddle. The stallion reared up and kicked out at the night air as if trying to defend its master from the unseen attackers.

Helplessly, Iron Eyes rolled and fell from the tall horse like a limp rag doll. His thin, emaciated frame crashed heavily into the sand. Within a few seconds the sand darkened as blood spread from his head where he lay motionless upon it.

The terrified stallion reared up over and over and lashed out with its hoofs. It was a pathetic sight which only served to make the pair of bush-whackers even more confident that they had achieved their goal.

Even from the distance between them both the outlaws could see no movement from the infamous bounty hunter. Iron Eyes lay like a corpse upon the blood-sodden sand.

Jones cranked the mechanism of his Winchester and sent a spent casing flying from its magazine. His partner duplicated the action. They moved forward and studied their joint handiwork. The closer they got the more irate the spirited horse became. The palomino stallion charged towards the outlaws, sending them fleeing back into the cover of the dense thicket of Joshua trees.

'That's one mad horse, pard,' Jones remarked.

'It surely is.'

21

Jones rubbed his dry mouth. 'Sure would like to own that animal but I got me a feeling he'd kill us if we even tried to get close to either him or that body.'

Hyams nodded in agreement, smiling.

'Who needs a big horse anyway? The most important thing is that we just killed Iron Eyes,' Hyams gloated as he looked across the quartermile distance between themselves and their victim. 'Now we ain't got to worry. Now we can head on to Twin Forks and have us some fun.'

Buster Jones grinned. 'Yep, there ain't nobody else gonna follow us.'

'I seen his head explode,' Hyams chuckled. 'Did you see it, Buster?'

'Yep, I seen the blood too.' Jones shrugged and turned to where they had left their mounts. 'That couldn't have been Iron Eyes though, Joe.'

'Why not?'

'Coz they reckon he can't be killed and we just killed that critter.' Jones pushed his rifle back into its scabbard and stepped into his stirrup. 'I figure that was an Apache.'

'Apaches never ride big horses like that 'un,' his partner disagreed. 'Not with fancy Mexican saddles. Whether you like it or not we just killed Iron Eyes.'

'Whoever he was he's dead.'

Hyams threw himself on to his own saddle, gathered his reins in his gloved hands and pushed his smoking rifle into its leather scabbard beneath his saddle. 'Do you figure we should go check that he is dead?'

Jones shook his head. 'No need. He's dead. Nobody gets shot in the head and lives, Joe. Besides, that damn crazy horse will rip our mounts apart if'n we even try.'

Hyams grinned and triumphantly slapped his partner's back as they steered their horses through the dense forest of thorns. 'Reckon you're right, pard.'

'Let's go drink that town dry.'

Both the wanted outlaws laughed out

loud and spurred their horses hard. The riders emerged from their hiding-place on to the sandy trail and headed on towards the remote border town.

* ★ ★

The sound of the two horses galloping off towards Twin Forks washed over the supine bounty hunter. Somehow defying his horrendous wound Iron Eyes opened his eyes and stared up at the bright moon.

He vainly tried to move but every ounce of wind had been kicked from his lean frame as he made impact upon the unforgiving ground.

Eventually he was able to turn his head. His eyes saw the blood that had stained the sand beside him.

'Damn. That ain't good,' he muttered feebly. Then he noticed a sound that he recognized. It tormented him. It was a sound inside his head.

Iron Eyes had heard the exploding drums before, and he did not like it one little bit. He was listening to his own heart pumping blood from a head wound.

'I gotta stop the bleeding fast,' the bounty hunter mumbled as he felt pain race through him. Every bruise was screaming out as he tried to move.

He blinked hard until his eyes began to see clearly again. His bony right hand went to his aching head and felt the deep gash that had been torn across his scalp. Each movement seemed to make the pounding of the war drums inside his skull grow louder.

Iron Eyes winced as his fingers touched the savage injury. He lowered his arm.

He focused on his fingertips and stared at the blood. It dripped from his long, thin digits like water. He placed his hand on his chest and then remembered the rifle smoke. A fury filled his heart.

'Now I'm real angry,' Iron Eyes muttered as the stallion moved above him and looked down. He reached out

25

and vainly tried to grab hold of the horse's bridle. The palomino snorted and raised its head. The bounty hunter's arm fell back down beside him. Everything inside his head was spinning and he could not stop it. He was caught in a whirlpool. Every instinct inside his pounding mind told him he had to stem the flow of blood if he were to survive. But how?

Iron Eyes was being sucked down into an ocean of his own blood. He was going to drown unless he could get up off his back and tend to his wound.

The drumming grew deafening.

His eyes closed again.

He attempted to remain conscious, yet no matter how hard he fought Iron Eyes knew that he could not win this battle. All he could do was hang on, ride the waves and hope that his strength returned to his long, thin body.

The infamous hunter of men mustered all of his energy and forced himself up into a sitting position. For a moment he felt as though he had beaten the odds, but then he felt himself falling backwards once more.

He collapsed on the blood-soaked sand. The Devil had roped him and was hauling him down towards the bowels of Hell.

Iron Eyes was falling into a black abyss. It was an unholy place where no angels dared to venture.

It was a land from where most did not return.

2

In the darkness of night the border towns sparkled like jewels set along an invisible chain: a necklace that stretched as far as the eye could see in either direction. They were like beacons luring the drifting riders out of the black prairies to places where they knew they could find anything they desired. Hard liquor and soft women was a combination all men with blood flowing through their veins craved after surviving the desolation of the unforgiving trail.

Every town was different yet they all provided the same basic necessities to keep men sane. This was not an easy land to travel through, and as almost the entire border was unmarked the law was virtually ineffectual. No one knew for sure which country they were in, let alone what laws they should be obeying.

The majority of the inhabitants of the settlements dotted at intervals along the border decided to ignore them all. It was a lot easier that way. Only when there were heavily armed men with tin stars pinned to their vests did anyone give the law a second thought.

Yet even a heavily notched gun grip did not impress most of the hardened souls who travelled this part of the country.

The majority of the drifters who roamed from town to town were more than capable and willing to shoot their way out of any argument. Even tin stars could never protect a man from the deadly wrath of those who lived by their own brand of law.

Gun law.

Soon blood would be spilled again, as was the nightly ritual. It was only a matter of where and when in the sprawling town.

A white-faced clock set high on a church tower told everyone who happened to look upwards that it was close to midnight. Yet few among the growing crowd that filled the streets of the town set on the border ever glanced upwards. Their eyes were focused on other things. Santa Rosa was filled with men sporting holstered guns and it paid to be aware of each and every one of them.

Dust rose up into the evening lantern light off the hoofs of the tall grey quarter horse as its master steered it down through the narrow side streets towards the centre of the busy town.

Santa Rosa was by far the busiest of all the border towns and as it grew ever darker the sprawling settlement became even busier and louder.

None of this bothered the grim-faced rider sitting astride his high-shouldered mount. His eyes sought just one face and ignored all of the others.

Whatever his true name was he had only ever answered to the name of Wolfe. He had once been a famed gunfighter and had earned top dollar hiring out his lethal talents to anyone who could afford his fee. For years he had done other men's killing for them and earned himself a small fortune.

Then he had encountered Iron Eyes and learned the hard way that there was always someone faster with a gun. Wolfe had made just one mistake in his well-planned bushwhacking of an innocent rancher. He had not considered what the infamous bounty hunter might do when he suddenly rode into the middle of the action.

Iron Eyes had taken the side of the unarmed rancher and defended the wounded man, not only with his own life but with his Navy Colts.

It had been the first time in his entire life that Wolfe had tasted lead. The brutal battle between the two men had lasted no more than five minutes but it had left Wolfe with his right arm nearly sheared from his body by lethally accurate bullets.

Iron Eyes had crippled the hired gunman and left him for dead. But, against all the odds, Wolfe did not die.

31

He did vow to get even, though, and that was why he was here in Santa Rosa. He was here to find the man who had crippled him. Find and kill Iron Eyes. It was his driving force and nothing could stop him.

His spurs encouraged the grey down towards the bright street illumination. The hundreds of faces that glanced in his direction meant nothing to him.

They were not the faces of the man he hunted.

That scarred face was branded into his mind for all time.

The tall grey mount nervously moved out into the middle of the main street. A score of horses were tethered to hitching rails to either side of the unlit alleyway from which it had just emerged. Men and women alike seemed unaware of the stranger in their midst. If any of them had realized how dangerous Wolfe was they might not have showed him their backs.

The middle of Santa Rosa was full of people rejoicing at the coming of another night. The sound of a hundred guitars blended with tinny pianos. Lantern light shone and music tinkled from every open saloon doorway out into the street yet the one-armed rider did not seem to notice anything but what lay directly ahead of his lathered-up mount.

There was only one thing on the mind of the grim-faced horseman: finding and killing the man he blamed for his misfortune.

He had invested nearly two years of his life in hunting down the infamous Iron Eyes. Wolfe had come close to catching up with the bounty hunter only a few months before. He had been about to strike when his horse had broken a leg in full flight. By the time he had managed to walk back to the nearest settlement and buy a new mount Iron Eyes and his strange female companion known as Squirrel Sally were long gone. Wolfe cursed his misfortune, but his failure had only fuelled his urge to continue his deadly quest.

Wolfe could never stop hunting the

one man who had not only outdrawn him but had also left him crippled.

He had to avenge that wrong.

It had taken the deadly gunfighter six months to learn how to use his left hand and draw his Colt Peacemaker after his right arm had been amputated two years earlier. Wolfe knew that he was never going to be the man he had once been, but that did not matter to him. All that mattered was killing Iron Eyes and letting everyone know about it. He knew that the man who killed the infamous bounty hunter would gain a reputation worth its weight in gold coin.

Once again he would become the highest paid hired killer in the West, for anyone who managed to kill Iron Eyes could name their own price.

Suddenly a few shots rang out. Wolfe looped his long leathers around his saddle horn and swiftly drew his six-shooter from his custom-made holster.

In one swift action he had not only drawn but cocked his gun. His eyes narrowed as he stared to where he saw a pair of drunken cowboys waving their weapons in the air.

Wolfe released the hammer of his .45 and pushed it back into his holster. He took the reins and turned the horse and jabbed his spurs again. The grey walked slowly through the crowded street as its master continued to search the area for his prey.

Iron Eyes had to be close, Wolfe kept silently telling himself. He eased back on his reins and studied Santa Rosa's main street. There were so many people but none of them looked remotely like Iron Eyes.

Revenge had driven him on when most sane souls would have quit and admitted defeat. There was a burning fire inside the gunfighter, which only killing Iron Eyes could extinguish. He blamed Iron Eyes for many things but most of all Wolfe blamed the notorious bounty hunter for the loss of his right arm. He recalled how he had lost count of how many bullets had torn into his flesh. His arm had almost been severed.

No one could shoot like that, except Iron Eyes. Wolfe inhaled through his flared nostrils and continued to study the street and its occupants.

Where was he? The question burned into the horseman.

Whilst Iron Eyes had hunted those wanted dead or alive for the bounties on their heads, Wolfe had ridden relentlessly across two territories just to try and catch up with his prey before killing him.

In his mind Wolfe had killed Iron Eyes in a thousand different ways. He had killed him quickly with bravado. He had bushwhacked the bounty hunter. He had killed Iron Eyes slowly and even considered the satisfaction of torturing the man he hated.

There were so many options.

It grieved Wolfe that he would only be able to kill Iron Eyes once. Creatures like him deserved to be killed more than once, he told himself.

He eased the grey mount towards the

nearest boardwalk as a buckboard, pulled by a massive chestnut horse, moved through the crowd towards him. A sleeping man with an empty whiskey bottle between his legs sat on its driving board.

Suddenly his horse shied as dozens of sombrero-wearing men flooded from a cantina behind the tail of his grey and headed towards the nearest saloon. His powerful left arm dragged back on his reins and held the animal in check until it calmed down.

Again Wolfe swung his horse around and searched the street for any hint of the man he sought. Even though the street was filled to overflowing with men, women and horses there seemed to be no sign of Iron Eyes.

That confused Wolfe.

For two long weeks Wolfe had followed the tracks of the battered old stagecoach that he knew Squirrel Sally drove. The wheel tracks had led to this very town.

It seemed obvious to the gunfighter

that if he found the stagecoach he would also find its owner. When he found Squirrel Sally he would also find her man.

He would, in the end, find Iron Eyes.

Then the shooting would start again. Then their war would come to its indubitable conclusion. This time it would not be Iron Eyes who was the victor. Wolfe sneered and nodded. This time it would be the bounty hunter who ended up riddled with lead.

Wolfe aimed the grey towards a hitching rail without any horses tied to its weathered pole. His ruthless stare focused on the sign nailed just over the large window and door.

'Funeral Parlour,' Wolfe read aloud. He smiled.

He was about to dismount when something familiar caught his attention a hundred yards along the street. It was something bathed in the light of hanging lanterns.

For a few moments Wolfe did not believe his own eyes as he focused hard through the amber lantern light which filled the street. Then he slowly began to realize that his eyes were not playing tricks on him but actually telling him the truth.

Wolfe rested his left hand on his saddle horn, rose up and balanced in his stirrups. A cruel smile broke over his unshaven features.

'The stagecoach,' Wolfe whispered and sat back down on his high saddle.

He wrapped his reins around his wrist and drew his gun. His thumb cocked its hammer until it locked fully into position.

Like a man possessed by demons Wolfe leaned forward and spurred the grey viciously. The powerful quarter horse reacted immediately and raced towards the stationary stagecoach.

It did not matter to Wolfe how many innocent people were trampled beneath his horse's hoofs. All that mattered to the determined rider was getting to the stagecoach that he knew belonged to the female who claimed to be Iron

Eyes's woman. The grey charged, with its master balanced like a tightrope walker on its saddle.

The horse carved a path through the crowd as Wolfe held his weapon at arm's length. Startled men and women leapt to safety as the horseman drove his mount through them towards the stagecoach.

The one-armed horseman somehow controlled his galloping mount with only his muscular legs.

As he got within twenty yards of the long vehicle the crowd around it had dispersed. Wolfe hauled back on his reins and stopped the grey. A cloud of dust billowed up from the dry ground, stirred by the hoofs of the snorting horse.

When the choking dust cleared Wolfe was standing beside the high-shouldered animal with his cocked six-shooter still held in his hand at the end of his outstretched arm.

His eyes darted from shadow to shadow in search of an answer to where either Squirrel Sally or Iron Eyes were. He strode towards the stagecoach and looked into its interior.

'Where are they?' Wolfe growled.

3

The livery stable was set at the far end of Santa Rosa's main thoroughfare. It was a tall, wide, weathered structure with huge double doors and a hay loft directly above them. A joist with a pulley and hook jutted out over the open loft space.

Wolfe moved around the stagecoach with his mount in tow towards the open doorway. With each determined step his eyes continued vainly to search the area for any hint of those he sought.

The inside of the livery stable was well illuminated. A few oil lanterns and a glowing blacksmith's forge filled the spacious interior with a strange warm light.

Wolfe walked into the stables, then abruptly halted when he heard a noise to his right. He dropped on to one knee and pointed the seven-inch barrel of his

Peacemaker to where he had heard the sound.

'Don't shoot.' A voice echoed around the cavernous interior of the livery stable. 'I ain't got me no guns.'

'Who are you?' Wolfe asked. He rose slowly to his full height.

A man ambled out from the shadows. He was well built and his sweating skin reflected the dancing lantern light.

'I'm the blacksmith, mister,' the man said fearfully as he raised his arms in submission. 'My name's Jack.'

'I don't give a damn what your name is,' Wolfe hissed like a sidewinder and strode towards the blacksmith. 'You know anything about that stagecoach outside your door?'

'Sure do.'

'Well?' Wolfe rammed the barrel of his gun into the man's belly.

'A female give me a fifty-dollar gold piece to tend her team earlier.' The blacksmith gulped. He pointed to his stalls where all six of her horses were stabled. 'There they are.'

Wolfe gritted his teeth. 'Where is the little gal?'

'She went to one of the hotels,' the man replied. 'She was real messy. Reckon she was gonna get herself a bath and some shut-eye.'

Wolfe turned away from the man. He looked at the team of six horses, then his eyes returned to the shaking blacksmith.

'What about her companion?'

'Her what?'

'What about the man she was travelling with?' Wolfe snarled. 'A tall, thin critter with long hair like an Apache. What about him? Where'd he go?'

Jack Carson looked bewildered, because he was. 'There weren't no man with that little gal, mister. Honest. She was on her lonesome.'

'Alone?' Wolfe was thoughtful. 'How could she be alone? That don't make any sense.'

'She gave me a fifty-dollar golden piece to tend these nags and told me to keep the change,' the nervous blacksmith repeated. 'She had a whole bag of them. I never seen so much gold coin in all my days. I wonder where she got all that money from?'

'You don't wanna know.' Wolfe walked around the interior of the livery stable. He studied every horse in each of the stalls. Then he stopped and turned back. The spring had gone from his step as his mind raced.

'What you looking for?' the blacksmith asked.

'I'm looking for a big palomino stallion with a Mexican saddle,' Wolfe muttered as he reached the forge and allowed its heat to warm his bones. He released the hammer of his Peacemaker and slid it into the holster he wore across his middle.

'I ain't seen a palomino for the longest time.'

Wolfe exhaled. 'Did the female happen to mention anything about her man?'

The blacksmith nodded. 'Now you mention it she did kinda bend my ear about some varmint she said she was betrothed to. What was his name?'

'Iron Eyes.'

'Yep, that was it.'

'What did she say about him?'

The blacksmith looked up at the rafters. 'She said that he was someplace else and she had to travel there after she'd rested up her team.'

'Exactly where did she say Iron Eyes was?'

Wolfe raised an eyebrow.

'Twin Forks,' the large man recalled.

'Where the hell is that?'

'Ten miles east of here.'

Wolfe looked at the blacksmith, then pointed at his grey. 'Tend my horse. Wash him down and feed and water him. I want him ready to ride by sunrise.'

'Should I tell the little gal that you was asking after her, mister?' the large man asked as he took hold of the grey's bridle and began to lead it into the livery.

Wolfe shook his head. 'Nope.'

The blacksmith watched as the

one-armed man walked out into the street. He gave out a long sigh as he began to sense how close he had just come to dying.

4

A hundred sounds all competed with one another inside the head of the unconscious bounty hunter. Each was different from the next. Each fought and tried to dominate the man who should have been dead and yet somehow was still in the land of the living. They grew louder and more intense. These were not noises created by a damaged brain but by other things. Things which were alive and somewhere close to his helpless form.

The delirious mind of the bloodsoaked Iron Eyes started to defeat the talons of death which had been clawing at him since he had been hit by the rifle bullet.

His arms and legs lashed out as though fighting some unseen enemy. He reached up and grabbed at the throat of his concerned mount and gripped its bridle.

The stallion raised its neck and head and Iron Eyes clung on. The sounds became louder as his bullet-coloured eyes opened.

Iron Eyes looked through the limp strands of hair and saw the coyotes not more than twenty yards away from him. He was on his knees and the horse was trying to jerk its head up as its master hung on to its bridle.

The coyotes were baying at the moon. The vicious wild dogs were giving thanks for the presenting of an unexpected meal. Iron Eyes managed to place his right boot heel on the sand and steadied his weak body. Somehow he dragged his other leg up and placed the boot next to the other.

He kept hold of the bridle with both of his bony hands as his horse snorted. He was confused but started to realize that the sounds which had managed to penetrate his delirium were those of the coyotes and his protective horse.

Iron Eyes swallowed hard. The

magnificent stallion had saved his life once again, he reasoned. He was rocking like a drunkard and could feel the blood still dripping from the brutal wound on to his shoulder.

He still needed to stop the bleeding, he told himself, but there was another more urgent problem.

The coyotes had followed the scent of his blood to this spot and they were not going to be easily talked out of a meal.

His eyes darted from one animal to the next. Drool ran from all of their fang-filled mouths. They were ready to strike at both the bounty hunter and the horse.

Iron Eyes released the grip of his right hand from the bridle and lowered it down to his waist where one of his Navy Colts was still jammed in behind his belt buckle against his flat belly.

The fingers of the bony hand curled around the grip of the deadly gun. Iron Eyes pulled it free and dragged its hammer back until it locked.

The .36 had never felt so heavy.

Iron Eyes had to use all his strength to raise his arm and aim in the direction of the four coyotes. The moonlight was playing tricks with his weary eyes.

The animals were growling now.

They were also fanning out in the way he had seen wolves do when trying to confuse their prey.

Iron Eyes kept hold of the horse's bridle with one hand as he swayed on his heels and fought to aim his gun. Then he began to wonder if there were actually four of the wild dogs facing him down.

He knew he might actually be seeing double, or not seeing their true number at all.

Iron Eyes blinked hard again and narrowed his eyes.

Were there four targets, or five or six?

What if there were only two?

Which did he shoot at? What if he wasted bullets and actually shot the air between them? Would they turn and run or would they attack? Suddenly, without warning, each of the animals let

51

out a spine-chilling growl and started to race towards the bounty hunter and his mount.

His arm was shaking as he held the gun at hip height.

Defiantly, Iron Eyes fired over and over again. Acrid gunsmoke filled the air. His gun was empty as he felt one of the coyotes fall at his boots. He pushed the smoking gun down into his deep trail-coat pocket and glared through the smoke at the wounded coyote. The animal was not quite dead. Iron Eyes reached down and pulled out his Bowie knife from the neck of his boot.

The bounty hunter leaned over and thrust the long blade of his knife into the heart of the snarling wild dog. The coyote stopped growling. Iron Eyes used his grip on the horse's bridle to straighten up, then he wiped the knife across his sleeve.

The smoke cleared and allowed him to see the dead coyotes.

Iron Eyes staggered to his saddle-bags, withdrew a bottle of whiskey and pulled its cork with his teeth. He spat it at the dead animals and poured the fiery liquor over the blade of his knife.

'This is gonna hurt,' he told himself. He took a long swallow of the whiskey and placed the bottle back in the bag carefully. 'I'll drink the rest of you when I've stopped this damn bleeding.'

He leaned his skeletal frame against the horse and pulled out a twisted cigar from his pocket.

He rammed the black weed into the corner of his mouth and struck a match with his thumb-nail.

The match erupted and was raised to the whiskey-sodden knife blade. Iron Eyes watched as the bluish flame engulfed the Bowie knife in his hand. He raised it to the end of his cigar and inhaled the smoke.

Then closing his eyes he placed the blade against the wound on the side of his head. The pain was worse than any he had ever endured before. Iron Eyes wanted to pull the blade away but knew he had to keep it there until the blood stopped pouring from the horrific gash. He could smell his hair and flesh burning as the hot knife-edge did its work and melted the skin along the deep bullet wound.

The knife fell and landed in the sand by his boots. He raised his shaking hand and patted the smoking side of his head until he was sure he had extinguished the flames. Only then did he exhale the smoke which had been trapped in his lungs.

Somehow his long, thin hand found the neck of the whiskey bottle again and he pulled it from the saddlebag. He spat the cigar away and lifted the bottle to his lips.

He started to drink.

He would not stop until the bottle was empty.

5

Every night was a fiesta along the border. The bustling streets of Santa Rosa were still filled with the sounds of music and countless people moving from one saloon and gambling hall to the next. The night was still young and along the border the coming of darkness meant only one thing. It meant seeking and finding pleasure wherever it might be before dawn returned and ended another night's revelry. The amber lantern light bathed the long wide main street in a deceptively tranquil glow that tended to make everything appear less dangerous than under the unrelenting rays of the daytime sun.

Yet in truth darkness never provided anything except shadows where the most evil of creatures tended to lie in wait for the unwary.

Set midway along the wide street a handful of well-constructed stores, in total contrast to the saloons and gambling halls, did slow but steady business. A barber-shop, which never seemed to close its doors, rubbed shoulders with both a printer's and a far more imposing bathhouse.

The bathhouse was a large two-storey building where males and females were channelled up separate staircases to bathe with their own gender. Steam filled the building as large boilers at the rear of the ground floor worked furiously to provide hot water for its patrons.

For the first time in weeks Squirrel Sally was clean and dressed in a fresh shirt and pants as she came down the staircase to where men and women sat waiting for their turn to wash away their sins. The young female in the ill-fitting trail gear almost glowed as she reached the lobby. For the first time since she had been forced to leave her distant home she had been able to wash the grime from her petite frame.

Travelling with the infamous Iron Eyes was something few could have ever managed. It was a hard way to live and yet for some unknown reason she had chosen it.

Unlike all others who set eyes upon the bounty hunter Squirrel Sally did not see the hideous scars that had mutilated his features. She did not see the dried bloodstains that covered his torn and ragged clothing. Whatever it was she saw, it was buried deep beneath the battle-scarred surface of the man called Iron Eyes.

Sally only saw the soul of the strange hunter of men and in her own way she loved him. Yet no matter how hard she had tried she had so far failed to ignite a spark of desire or interest in him. It seemed as though the accumulation of his bloody injuries had made him mistrust anyone who showed any hint of kindness towards him.

To most it would have seemed like a futile exercise but the feisty female would never quit until he eventually succumbed. Young as she was, Sally had chosen her mate and would not rest until she caught him in her relentless feminine web. He might be incapable of understanding it but Iron Eyes was her man and one day he would be able to accept that fact.

Sally smelled of perfumed soap as she held her canvas bag under her arm and balanced her prized Winchester on her slender shoulder. She felt like a princess as her bare feet stroked the carpeted staircase beneath them. Sally had booked her room in the hotel across the street before being lured into the bathhouse.

For the first time in months she had allowed her femininity to overrule her head. There was no profit in being clean, but as she inhaled the smell of the scented soap that followed her across the lobby, she realized that profit was not everything.

Sometimes a girl had to indulge herself. Sally hoped the scent of the perfumed soap would last until she once again met up with Iron Eyes.

Her eyes sparkled like jewels in the lantern light. There was more than one way to bait a trap, she thought, as an impish smile illuminated her beautiful, unspoiled face.

She stepped out of the brightly lit bathhouse on to the boardwalk and paused. There were still far more people wandering the street than horses. There were still so many people it was hard for her to see across the street. She opened her bag, pulled out a cigar, poked it into the corner of her mouth and then searched for a match.

A tall shadow fell across her petite form. For a brief moment her heart raced. Had Iron Eyes returned? Her head tilted and she looked through her clean golden locks up at the unfamiliar figure.

'Let me light that for you, darling.' A tall cowboy touched his hat brim before he ran a match down the porch upright and cupped its flame. He stepped closer with the sheltered flame.

It flickered as she frowned with disappointment. This was not the man she wanted to see. He was not Iron Eyes. Whoever he was, he was not her beloved bounty hunter.

'You'd best be quick,' the cowboy said as he saw the flame of his match getting closer to his finger-tips.

Squirrel Sally shrugged. She leaned forward and sucked in the smoke of her cigar. She was curious as to why a total stranger would talk to her. Like so many attractive creatures, she had no idea that she was beautiful and a temptation to all men with warm blood flowing through their veins.

'Thank you kindly,' she said before blowing out a long line of smoke. He dropped the blackened sliver of wood and continued to feast his eyes on her. She expected him to carry on to wherever it was he was headed but he remained standing beside her. She could see him from the corner of her eye glaring down at her.

'You sure are pretty,' the cowboy said. 'You even smell pretty.'

'I just had me a bath,' Sally said, and sighed through a cloud of smoke.

He rubbed his hands together. 'I can just see you lying in a tub all naked and rubbing your skin with bubbles and all.'

Sally turned her head briefly and frowned at him. 'You want something?'

Of all the questions she could have asked the cowboy Sally had chosen the wrong one. It was as if she had invited him to get friendly. Far friendlier than she had ever imagined was possible. He moved towards her. He was a cowboy and he was wrangling a mare. Wherever she moved he managed to block her progress with expert ease.

She stopped and glared up at his grinning face. If looks could kill the cowboy was a dead man.

'I'm starting to get real angry with you,' she said bluntly. 'If you had half a brain you'd quit before I hurt you.'

The cowboy laughed out loud.

'I sure like me a gal with grit.'

61

Squirrel Sally tilted her head and stared blankly up into his eyes. She had seen that very same look in the faces of a lot of men since her tiny body had developed from that of a young girl into that of a young woman. She inhaled the cigar smoke and angrily blew it into the cowboy's face.

There were few females anywhere close to the unmarked border who were quite as volatile as Squirrel Sally Cooke. Her temper was well known to those whom she had encountered since she had first wounded Iron Eyes. His back still bore the scar of a rifle bullet that she had fired at him. Although innocently pretty and very small she was more than a match for anyone when she was riled. The drunken cowboy did not know it but his unwelcome advances had confused her, and when Sally was confused she was dangerous.

Mighty dangerous.

'Listen up, you're making a real big mistake.' Sally turned away from the amorous cowboy and then warned,

'You're heading for a whole heap of pain.'

The cowboy lunged at her.

'Come here, you little vixen. I know a tease when I set eyes on one. I'm gonna teach you a lesson.' He grabbed and swung her around to face him. He was no longer thinking with his brain but with another more visible organ.

As she came to an abrupt halt and was jerked almost off her feet by the violent action her cigar went flying from her lips. Sally blew the long damp strands of hair away from her eyes and looked up into the cowboy's lecherous face. She was bewildered and even though she was angry she was unsure what she should do.

This was something she had never experienced before.

'What in tarnation are you doing?' Sally gasped in total shock. For like so many other females she did not understand that a certain breed of men preyed upon those they deemed were incapable of defending themselves or their virtue.

To the predator she was an easy target. Even the rifle she carried did not alarm the cowboy, because all he saw was a tiny female who could never protect herself against anyone as big and strong as he was.

It was a mistake. A big one.

His sap was rising. He was like a thirsty man faced with a pitcher of ice-cold beer. He threw her against the wall where the shadows could hide his actions from those who were still filling the street. Unaware of what the cowboy actually wanted from her, Sally held on to her rifle and bag as if they were the most precious things she possessed.

He forced her backwards. 'I'll show you the best time you ever had, little missy.'

Sally could feel the wooden wall at her back. She also felt the rifle in her left hand. She defiantly smiled at him as a deadly thought raced through her young mind.

What would Iron Eyes do?

If this was an outlaw the bounty

hunter would simply kill him. She wanted to kill the cowboy but knew that might not be the right thing to do. Sally pondered the problem as she struggled to get free.

The more she fought the more he leaned over her. He was heavy and was well used to using his weight to overpower those smaller than himself. Sally began to realize that he had done this before to girls less able than she was to protect themselves.

That riled her.

'Get off me,' Sally said, and snorted.

'You know you like it, gal,' the cowboy said, trying to kiss her whilst she was pinned against the wall. 'Quit fighting and enjoy yourself.'

There was only one man she would entertain doing what this cattle-roper was attempting to do. The cowboy was not that man.

Sally felt his rough hands moving all over her young body and she did not like it. He was quick, she thought. His hands seemed to move to each of her most private places faster than she could defend herself.

'Holy cow,' Sally snarled angrily. 'How many damn hands have you got anyway?'

'Let's go in the alley,' the cowboy hissed into her ear. 'I'll show you I got me other things besides my hands I can use to pleasure a gal.'

She had always been good when it came to wrestling but she was losing this contest. Then she realized that she was hampered by her heavy canvas bag as well as her grip on her prized Winchester. She dropped the bag. Its hefty contents thudded on the board-walk at her bare feet.

She felt him push her up against the wall with the weight of his excited body. Her eyebrows rose. She could feel his excitement right through her clothing. There was only one man she had ever wanted to experience this sort of thing with and he was far away, hunting two wanted outlaws.

'Let go or I'll stomp you,' Sally

growled as he forced her towards the narrow gap between the bathhouse and the barber-shop.

He did not listen. He just kept using his superior strength to move her to where no one could see what he intended to do.

'Trust me, missy. You're gonna love it. You might even thank me.' The cowboy had drunk just enough hard liquor to make him adventurous.

Squirrel Sally frantically fought his large hands as they fumbled with her shirt buttons. He was far bigger and stronger than she was, and Sally was smart enough to realize that she could not win this fight on his terms. She had to use her diminutive size and speed to get the better of him.

'Well, you asked for it, sweetheart, and I'm gonna let you have it,' Sally whispered seductively into his ear. Her tone made him pause for a fraction of a second. That was all the time she required.

Faster than he had seen anyone ever

move before Sally ducked under his arm and left him groping the wall. She stood with her bare feet a few feet apart and bounced up and down like a prizefighter waiting to throw a knock-out punch. But it was not to administer a punch that she was steadying herself. It was something far more personal and devastating.

The cowboy smiled and ominously turned to face her. He thought she was playing but Sally was deadly serious.

'C'mon. Fight me if you can,' Sally taunted.

Her bare feet bounced up and down on the boardwalk before his lustful stare. She knew exactly what she was doing. She watched his eyes focusing on her chest as it moved unhindered by any civilized undergarment inside her shirt.

The cowboy was transfixed by the sight a mere few feet away from him. It was like a matador's cape taunting a rampant bull. He could not take his eyes from her barely concealed bosom, but he should have been concentrating on her small bare feet.

'You sure are one hell of a wildcat.' He sighed longingly at her as he readied himself to lunge again. 'I want you so damn bad it hurts.'

'I reckon this'll hurt a whole lot more, cowboy,' she snarled, and spat into his face. The cowboy turned his face aside. Sally sidestepped to the left and then back to the right. He clumsily tried to match her movement but Sally was far faster than he had ever been.

Then she stopped. With every ounce of her boundless energy she brought her bare foot up with painful accuracy. Her naked foot went between his legs with tremendous speed and force. She felt his manhood buckle inside his pants. There was a painful whimper as his head bowed down. She bounced back and watched his head come level with his belt buckle. Sally had hurt the cowboy but she had not finished.

Sally raced forward when his head was at its lowest. She smashed her knee into his face as hard as she could. The sound of teeth cracking sounded along the boardwalk as the cowboy arched back up.

Blood and teeth fell from his open mouth as the dazed cowboy staggered towards her. It was impossible for Sally to tell if he was still smiling. There was far too much blood covering his face.

He vainly tried to speak.

Now it was her turn to laugh.

'I ain't finished yet, cowboy,' Sally said.

Squirrel Sally juggled the rifle off her shoulder, grabbed its stock and viciously brought the Winchester's barrel across the side of his head.

The sound of the metal barrel colliding with his skull filled the porch. A few of the passing crowd glanced towards the bathhouse just in time to see the final act of a very short fight.

The cowboy went flying like tumble-weed off the boardwalk towards the street. His limp body hit the ground hard. It did not stop rolling until he crashed into a water trough.

A few of the people who had witnessed the David and Goliath scenario roared with laughter and continued on their merry way. A couple of them even applauded. Squirrel Sally inhaled deeply and gave a triumphant bow.

'Now I'm finished.' She nodded angrily as she glared down at his crumpled body. 'And so are you. It don't pay to mess with me.'

Sally plucked her heavy bag up off the boards and tucked it under her armpit. Then, as though nothing had happened she resumed her position on the edge of the boardwalk. Her toes curled around the wooden boards as she looked up and down the street.

Santa Rosa was a curiosity to the young female. She had never witnessed so many men and women so seemingly determined to enjoy themselves after dark as these people seemed to be.

Squirrel Sally wondered why. It looked like hard work.

Her beautiful eyes looked across at

the hotel where she had already booked a room for the night. The grand building was directly opposite her. She glanced into her canvas bag at the large pouch of gold coins Iron Eyes had given to her. A smile traced over her handsome features.

One day Iron Eyes would do what the cowboy lying in the shadow of the trough had done, she told herself. When the bounty hunter attempted that dangerous act, she would not fight.

Again she glanced at the unconscious cowboy.

'Hell, I warned you,' she said with a sigh and looked at her bruised toes. 'I'm betrothed and only one man can play with my chest and you ain't him.'

Sally was about to pull another cigar from the bag before stepping down from the boardwalk to navigate through the crowd towards the hotel when something to her right caught her honed attention.

When you were as skilled a hunter as she was you learned never to ignore even the slightest of movements. To do so could mean the difference between life and death in the wilderness. Santa Rosa might have been a really big town but Sally knew it was no safer than a forest filled with deadly wolves.

The young female paused and turned. Her keen eyes searched along the street.

Sally had no idea what she had seen out of the corner of her eye but would not be satisfied until she discovered the answer.

There were few cats as curious as Squirrel Sally Cooke.

The street was not as busy as it had been when she had entered the bathhouse but it was still full of people. She stretched to her full height of nearly five foot. Even at full stretch she was still shy of getting a clear view of the far end of the main street.

'Damn it all!' Sally cursed angrily. 'How's a gal meant to see anything over all them ten-gallon hats?'

The youngster then looked at the

horse trough. It was taller than the boardwalk she stood upon. An idea came to her. She stepped on to it and rested her hand against the closest porch upright.

Her toes curled around the edge of the trough as she squinted over the heads of those who were walking in various directions through the amber lantern light along the thoroughfare.

'What in tarnation did I see?' Sally asked herself as she began to doubt her well-honed instincts. 'I'm sure something caught my eye, but what?'

Her eyes darted at each and every one of the people who filled the street. There were so many of them and yet none of their faces looked remotely familiar.

Sally was about to admit defeat and jump back down when a cold shiver traced through her small body. She swallowed hard and stared at the figure a hundred yards up the street. It was like seeing a nightmare come to life.

Her heart was racing.

Suddenly Sally knew exactly what had alerted her survival instincts. He was not a man anyone tended to forget or ignore if they wanted to continue living.

There was no mistaking the one-armed man she had met only weeks before. Even with his back to her Sally recognized his gait. Few men she had ever met walked the way he did. It was branded into her memory for all time.

'Wolfe.' His name fell from her lips. It tasted like poison. Like a moth drawn to a naked flame she could do nothing but trail him. Sally jumped down to the sandy ground and cranked the rifle's mechanism until the Winchester was cocked. Something inside her kept telling her that she had to find out what he was doing in Santa Rosa.

She made her way through the crowd in pursuit of the haunting figure. Every sinew in her body was shaking with fear. Not fear for her own safety but fear for the man she loved.

Why was Wolfe here?

Was it just a coincidence or something far more lethal?

Sally wanted to warn Iron Eyes and yet she knew that it was impossible. The bounty hunter could be anywhere. He went where the trail of his prey led him.

Maybe Wolfe had done exactly the same thing, she thought. Maybe he had been following her stagecoach tracks to this place. Maybe Wolfe did not realize that Iron Eyes had already left Santa Rosa.

For the first time since she parted company with Iron Eyes she regretted her decision not to accompany the bounty hunter on his quest for the two outlaws. She moved back and forth through gaps in the crowd and caught brief glimpses of the man with one arm.

Like a hound on the trail of a raccoon, Sally continued after the one-armed man. With each step she kept mumbling the same question:

'What's Wolfe doing here?'

The problem was that Sally already knew the answer to her question. Wolfe had told her the answer on their previous encounter.

It was branded into her mind.

He was hunting Iron Eyes. For some unknown reason Wolfe was going to try and kill Iron Eyes.

Sally had no idea why but she continued to follow the man with one arm. There was a large saloon at the very end of the street. It was less ornate than those in the centre of the town and looked as though it catered for the settlement's unfortunate people who had less money in their pockets.

Sally studied the saloon as the bright moon illuminated its façade.

Its wooden walls still had flakes of ancient paint upon them but it had been a long time since anyone had attempted to protect the structure from the elements.

She wondered why Wolfe was heading to such a dilapidated saloon. He looked as if he could afford the finest whiskey in the best of Santa Rosa's numerous drinking holes. It was a mystery and Squirrel Sally intended getting to the root of it.

Sally paused at the corner of a storefront and watched Wolfe stride through the thinning crowd towards the saloon.

'There's something damn fishy about this,' she muttered and continued her pursuit.

6

Squirrel Sally did not allow the burden of carrying her rifle and the hefty canvas bag filled with gold coins either to deter her or slow her pace. The one-armed gunfighter had not turned round once since she had started trailing him. Sally was confident that he was totally unaware that she was following him.

But the youngster had yet to learn that there were many ways for someone to see what was stalking them without turning their head. Countless panes of glass set in windows and doors reflected everything. All main streets in towns and cities everywhere had their avenues of mirrors. They betrayed those who were too innocent or naïve to realize that simple fact.

Wolfe strode on.

Was he aware that he was being

followed? Sally had not seen any hint that he had noticed her as she had weaved through the crowded street after him.

Eventually he reached the saloon. She watched as the mysterious Wolfe stepped up on to its boardwalk, pushed the swing doors apart and entered. Her eyes narrowed as the swing doors rocked on their hinges. Now she did not have to hide, she told herself.

Sally ran through the lantern light and found a shadow to pause in beside the saloon's front wall. It was close to an alley which ran alongside the building. Her young heart was pounding inside her tight-fitting shirt as she rested.

Every eye inside the saloon was glued to the stranger who had just entered. They had all seen men with missing limbs before but none who still looked quite as dangerous as Wolfe.

The gunfighter walked across the sawdust in a direct line towards the bar counter. Men and bar-girls scattered.

Each of them recognized trouble when they saw it and the ruthless Wolfe oozed trouble from every pore.

Wolfe reached the counter and rested his hand upon its wet surface. His eyes focused on the bartender and defied him to move a muscle.

'Whiskey,' Wolfe rasped and placed a silver dollar down.

The bartender filled a thimble glass with the amber liquor and watched as the gunfighter downed it in one swallow.

'Anything else, stranger?'

'Is the door to the alley unlocked?' Wolfe asked.

The bartender nervously nodded. 'Yep.'

Wolfe touched his hat brim and proceeded towards it.

The sound of guitars playing inside the saloon resumed. It filled the air above her long golden hair. Sally looked up at the open window above her head. Suddenly she could hear many voices competing with the stringed instruments again and wondered what had caused the momentary silence. Then she started to think of what reason the deadly Wolfe might have had to enter the most ramshackle saloon in Santa Rosa.

Perhaps he was like other men and could not exist for too long without savouring the taste of either whiskey or obliging females.

Maybe he had rented a room.

Sally prayed that that was it. If he was headed to his bed that would give her time to get her stagecoach hitched up and drive on out to warn Iron Eyes. Yet no matter how hard she tried to convince herself she simply did not believe that it would be that simple.

Wolfe was no ordinary man.

He was on a personal crusade which could only have one conclusion and that involved either Iron Eyes or himself being ripped to shreds by the other's bullets.

Whatever he was doing in Santa Rosa it involved death.

Huddled in the dark shadows, Squirrel Sally cradled her rifle in her small hands. Its barrel was sticky with the fresh blood of the cowboy upon it.

Sally wondered what she should do next. She turned and looked at the windows of the saloon. As with all drinking holes they were covered with elaborate paintwork to prevent innocent eyes looking inside.

There was only one way of seeing what was happening within the saloon, to discover what Wolfe was doing, and that was to go to the swing doors and peer in.

Squirrel Sally knew she ought to have had a plan, even a vague notion of what she should do next, but she could not think of anything. The saloon was set at the far end of Main Street. There were far fewer street lanterns here and fewer stores open for business. There were even fewer people wandering around, although the saloon sounded as if it were full.

She bit her lip. 'Think, Sally. Think.'

Should she throw caution to the wind and just boldly enter the saloon? She was about to move from the shadows and rush into the saloon when she suddenly realized that to do so would be to alert Wolfe of her presence in Santa Rosa.

There was a slim chance that Wolfe did not know she was in town, but if she marched into the saloon she would give the game away. If he was still hunting Iron Eyes the sight of her would tell him he was close to his prey.

'Think, Sally. Think,' she muttered again. The only thing that kept entering her mind was that she should have shot Wolfe when she had been trailing him to this place. But unlike a lot of other folks who were toting weaponry, Sally could never bring herself to shoot anyone in the back.

Sally straightened up. There was only one course of action and that was to bite the bullet and follow Wolfe into the busy saloon, she resolved.

Suddenly, as she was about to do just that, she felt the hair at the nape of her neck move. There was no mistaking the feel of a cold steel gun barrel.

Sally froze.

'Drop that rifle,' Wolfe said from behind her.

'And if I don't?' Sally asked.

Wolfe cocked the hammer of his .45. 'Then I'll blow your pretty little head off your shoulders.'

Sally dropped her rifle and her canvas bag. She swallowed hard and watched as the deadly gunman moved around her until he was facing her. He had the six-shooter aimed at her face and she could see it was fully loaded.

'You gonna kill me?' Sally asked.

'I might,' Wolfe responded in a low growl.

Sally leaned back against the wall. Even the shadows could not hide the brutal expression on his face. Unlike their previous meeting it was obvious that this time Wolfe meant business.

'When did you spot me?' she asked. 'I thought I'd tracked you real well, Wolfe. I was even down-wind so you wouldn't catch my scent.'

Wolfe pressed the gun barrel against

her temple and tilted his head as he studied her in a fashion similar to that of the cowboy a few moments earlier.

'I saw you when you walked out from the bathhouse,' he replied. 'I'd been waiting across the street for the longest while. You sure took a long time to wash the trail dust from your sweet little body.'

She frowned.

'You knew I was in town?'

'Yep, I sure did.' Wolfe looked her up and down as he kept the gun barrel firmly pressed against her head. 'I saw your stagecoach parked outside the livery hours back. It weren't hard to find out where you had gone. Tell me, where's your betrothed? The liveryman said you were alone. Are you?'

'I'm alone,' Sally answered.

'You're wearing more clothes than the last time we met,' Wolfe observed. 'Shame. I'd bet your body is real handsome with all the dirt washed off it.'

Sally blinked hard. 'Get your gun out

of my face and maybe we can talk about my body.'

The gunfighter lowered his chin and glared at her. She had seen many men when they were about to kill. Wolfe had the same expression carved into his rugged features.

'Quit stalling. Where's Iron Eyes?' Wolfe snarled.

'Why?'

Wolfe pushed the gun barrel against her temple. Sally winced with pain. Her head was trapped between his .45 and the saloon wall. It hurt.

'Why?' Wolfe repeated. 'Because I intend killing the bastard. That's why.'

Sally could feel the fury in his every word.

He jiggled the stump of his right arm. 'Iron Eyes did this to me. Left me to bleed to death, but I didn't die. I made me a pact with the Devil himself to let me get my revenge. That sweetheart of yours is gonna pay. Pay with his hide.'

'He left me,' Sally blurted out, and tried to look as though she was broken-hearted. 'He up and left me. Iron Eyes didn't like being betrothed and the worthless varmint just lit out with his tail between his legs. I ain't got no idea where the stinking critter is.'

Wolfe smiled and shook his head. 'You ain't a very good liar, Sally.'

'It's the truth, I tell you,' Sally insisted. 'He just left me like I was nothing. I hate him.'

Wolfe shook his head again. 'You're trying to protect him for some reason. Damned if I can figure out why. I know he's on the trail of some poor outlaw but I wanna know which way he headed. Which way did he go?'

Sally tried to look away from his constant stare but it was impossible. His gun had her pinned to the wall. 'I ain't got no idea where he went, Wolfe. Honest Injun. I ain't seen him for over a week.'

'Still lying to protect the scarecrow,' Wolfe snarled.

An idea suddenly came to her youthful mind. She could try and kick

88

Wolfe in the same place she had kicked the cowboy, she thought.

Wolfe pulled his gun away from her temple and then slashed it across the top of her head. The gun barrel skinned her scalp. She buckled in pain as a thin line of blood trailed through her golden hair and ran down her pretty face. She steadied herself.

'What you do that for?'

The one-armed gunfighter inhaled deeply.

'I saw what you did to that cowboy, Sally,' Wolfe said as he considered his options. 'I knew what you were thinking about. Now forget it.'

Squirrel Sally rubbed the blood from her face and gritted her teeth. She was now as angry as Wolfe.

'I'll never tell you which way Iron Eyes went, Wolfe. Not if you smash my skull into a pulp. If you wanna find him you'll have to do it on your lonesome. Savvy?'

Wolfe looked at her with cruel intention burning in his unblinking eyes.

'No problem. I already know that he's headed for Twin Forks. Right?'

Sally's jaw dropped. 'How'd you know that?'

'I didn't,' Wolfe grunted. 'It was just a guess but now, thanks to you, I know for sure. Twin Forks is the next town from here.'

'Damn your stinking hide. You tricked me.' She went to strike out at him but he kicked her back. Sally bounced off the unforgiving wall.

'You're riding with the wrong man,' Wolfe said as he ran the barrel of his .45 over her shapely shirt front. 'If you were as smart as you're pretty you'd know a real man when you see one.'

'I should have shot you when I had me the chance, Wolfe.' Sally was close to tears as the realization that she had betrayed Iron Eyes swept through her tiny form.

'But knowing where he is and drawing him out into the open are two different things,' Wolfe said ominously. 'Reckon there's only one thing I can do to get Iron Eyes in my gunsights, Sally.'

'What's that?' she hissed.

'This.' With the gun still gripped in his hand Wolfe punched the young female in the jaw. The blow was sharp and accurate. Her eyes rolled up under her eyelids. She was unconscious. Before she could fall he holstered his gun and leaned into her. Sally fell limply over his shoulder. He reached down and grabbed her bag, then straightened up. He kicked her Winchester under the boardwalk and turned to face the long street. His eyes focused through the lantern light at the large livery stable at the other end of the long thoroughfare.

He started to make his way towards it.

'I'm going to take you with me, Sally,' Wolfe told his unconscious captive. 'The thing is, when you're hunting a certain type of animal you gotta use the right bait to have a chance of catching the damn thing. I figure you're the only bait that can lure Iron

Eyes into my gunsights.'

The one-armed man walked unhindered through the crowd with the tiny female draped over his shoulder like a Mexican blanket.

No one in the crowd seemed either to notice or care. They had seen a lot worse than a one-armed man carrying a helpless female over his shoulder.

7

Iron Eyes poked the bloodstained cigar between his razor-sharp teeth and grunted as he somehow managed to haul his frame up on to the Mexican saddle. He had reclaimed his guns from the sand and reloaded them both. They weighed heavily in his deep trail-coat pockets as they rested amid the countless loose bullets the bounty hunter stored there. His long, thin fingers found a match in his shirt pocket and dragged it across the silver saddle horn. He brought the flickering flame up to the cigar and sucked in the smoke.

His lungs were filled with the strong smoke as he tossed the match away. Iron Eyes held the smoke deep inside his thin body for a few endless moments, then he let it filter through his teeth.

There was barely any shadow from either horse or rider as the moon was now directly overhead. Iron Eyes pulled out two bloodstained Wanted posters and used the moonlight to study the crude images of the outlaws. One of them had missed his target whilst the other had got lucky, Iron Eyes thought.

It did not matter to the bounty hunter which of them had nearly split his skull in half with his rifle bullet.

They would both pay the same price.

They would both die.

He carefully refolded the two posters and returned them to the deep coat pocket, beside one of his Navy Colts. He inhaled more cigar smoke and touched the fearsome wound above his ear. It would leave yet another brutal scar to add to all of the others.

His long fingers rubbed his temple. The war drums still pounded inside his skull as his bony hands teased the reins to his left and turned the powerful stallion round to face the trail which snaked through the forest of Joshua trees and brutal cactus.

His cold, bullet-coloured eyes stared

far ahead. They were focused far beyond the prairie brush to the distant glow of lights. He had been to this unholy land before and knew he had made a stupid mistake by riding straight down the throats of the outlaws he was hunting.

A damn kid who was wet behind the ears would have known better, Iron Eyes silently cursed as he jabbed his spurs into the flanks of his loyal horse.

The palomino started to trot as its master chewed on the cigar and concentrated on the lights he was now aiming his horse at.

The horse gained pace as the bounty hunter kept tapping his spurs in time with the pain inside his head. He was angry. Far angrier than he had been for months. His venom was not aimed at his prey but at himself.

In all his days as a hunter he had never taken the creatures he hunted for granted until now. Hyams and Jones were nothing special, he kept thinking as the stallion stretched its legs beneath his ornate saddle. They were just outlaws who were wanted dead or alive, but they had taught him a lesson.

He had underestimated them and that annoyed the lethal bounty hunter. There was one thing you never did and that was think you were smarter than the animal you were tracking.

As the cool air hit his bloodied features Iron Eyes began to regain his wits. He had finished off the last of his whiskey after cauterizing his skin over the bone of his skull.

Any normal man would have filled his belly with food in order to try and regain his strength and replenish the blood he had lost, but not Iron Eyes. He lived by another code. When he was hungry he drank as much whiskey as he could because for some strange reason he had never managed to become drunk. No matter how good or bad the whiskey was it was never strong enough to blunt his lethal determination.

The stallion started to gallop. Its master rose in his stirrups and balanced his emaciated, thin frame over the handsome saddle.

Although the flaming knife blade had burned a large chunk of his mane of black hair down to his scalp, there was still enough of it left to beat up and down on his shoulders.

The powerful horse beneath him had the scent of the town's water troughs in its nostrils. Its hoofs were tearing up the sandy trail as it somehow increased its incredible pace. It began the descent down from the thicket of thorny brush towards the settlement.

Unlike his mount, Iron Eyes had another scent in his flared nostrils. It was that of his prey. The two outlaws might have imagined that they had killed the man who was hunting them but they would soon be taught that Iron Eyes was not an easy man to kill.

His eyes were screwed almost shut as they focused on the bright lights of Twin Forks. He lifted his long leathers, whipped the cream-coloured rump of his horse and continued to urge it ever onward.

With each long stride of the palomino the bounty hunter felt his former strength returning to him. Not even the agonizing war drums which refused to stop pounding inside his head could stop him now. For Iron Eyes wanted to taste revenge. He wanted to savour its acrid flavour as he unleashed his own brand of retribution on those who had not been brave enough to face him.

Iron Eyes had always been dangerous but now he was also injured and there was no more terrifying foe than the infamous bounty hunter when he was wounded.

The bright overhead moon cast an eerie glow upon the arid landscape as the stallion continued to gallop across the sand trail. Iron Eyes was now like a crazed madman as he whipped the palomino mercilessly to find a pace that not even the most powerful of horses could ever have managed.

As the handsome animal and its monstrous rider galloped up over the crest of the high ridge Iron Eyes managed to shake the fog from his eyes. The smell of the whiskey fumes cleared his head as his skeletal hands controlled the muscular creature beneath him. Like a vulture waiting for something to die his eyes burned down at the trail left by the two outlaws' horses in the smooth sand. There was no mistaking the route Hyams and Jones had taken after they had fled the dense forest.

Even in the middle of the night nothing could hide the evidence from the eyes of the determined bounty hunter. The bright moon had betrayed him earlier and allowed the outlaws an easy target, but now the very same celestial orb had shown him exactly where they were headed.

Iron Eyes spurred the palomino on towards the distant lights of Twin Forks. That was where the moonlit tracks were heading and that was where the bounty hunter would follow. He could almost taste the acrid flavour of gunsmoke already.

The prized stallion tore up the arid

ground as it raced through the tracks the two outlaws had left in their wake.

Iron Eyes forged on. He had no other option, for when he set out after his chosen prey the infamous horseman was unable to stop until those he hunted were dead. Some said that it was to have the mark of death branded on to your very soul when the notorious Iron Eyes had your Wanted poster in his deep pockets.

There was no escaping his deadly retribution. There was nowhere to hide because he was the ultimate hunter and could seek you out wherever you tried to find sanctuary. Something drew him to the men he chased. It was as though he had a power that no other bounty hunter possessed. The power to reel in anyone he had selected to hunt.

For this was not a man like other men.

This was a creature created in the bowels of Hell by the Devil himself. He was a living corpse who had yet to find a grave deep enough to hold him.

Somehow even when he had suffered injuries that would have ended the life of most men, Iron Eyes not only survived but became even more dangerous.

It was as if he refused to die.

Most dying creatures instinctively realize when the end is near and succumb to the inevitable. It seemed as if Iron Eyes was incapable of accepting or even understanding that basic instinct.

Things only died when they were tired of living. He had said that so many times that he had grown to believe it. No matter how hideous his wounds or how much of his own blood he wore on his battle-weary trail gear, Iron Eyes continued on.

The massive horse kept following the trail towards Twin Forks. Its master was now only fuelled by whiskey, cigars and venomous revenge. That was all Iron Eyes required, for he had just one thought in his fevered mind. A thought that was sharper than his bloodstained spurs and drove him on.

It was to end this hunt and claim the reward money.

The outlaws did not know it yet but Death was following their trail. Death was riding closer and closer astride a palomino stallion.

Death would not be denied.

For its name was Iron Eyes.

8

With his matted mane of blood-covered hair hanging across his face and shoulders, Iron Eyes looked more dead than alive as his bony hands held on to his reins and steered the tall horse through the moonlight towards the flickering lights of the town. He was no longer standing in his stirrups as he approached the border town but slumped wearily over the saddle horn.

His injured body hurt as if a lightning bolt had torn through it. Yet there had been no storm apart from the one which raged inside his still dazed head.

Even the slightest action was now taking its toll on his already emaciated body. Each movement felt like arrows piercing his skeletal form. The only thing which kept him conscious was total willpower.

Willpower and anger.

His flared nostrils inhaled the scent of the town ahead of him. The scent of civilization was something Iron Eyes had never cared for, yet it had its uses. It alerted even the weariest of men when they were riding into a place where many other two-legged creatures lived.

His eyes darted about behind the veil of long limp strands of hair. He saw everything and did not miss any hint of danger which most might have ignored. That was how you survived in the West.

You looked and you listened.

He ran the back of his left hand across his mouth. He was far thirstier than he had ever been in all his days. He needed to fill his innards with whiskey, his mind kept nagging. He needed to rekindle his strength.

As always Iron Eyes was too stubborn to quit. Even death itself could not have prevented him from seeking revenge on the rifleman who had ripped the side of his head apart with a rifle bullet. For the umpteenth time he reached back and checked both satchels of each saddlebag in search for whiskey but there was none.

He had consumed it all, apart from the amount he had wasted setting the blade of his Bowie knife alight to burn his scalp into submission.

Iron Eyes looked ahead of him. The bullet-coloured eyes searched for the first place where he could buy more of the fiery liquor his embattled body craved.

The stallion walked on.

'I need me a saloon,' the bounty hunter whispered.

His long, thin fingers patted every pocket until they found another of his stale cigarillos. Like its predecessor it was covered in his blood.

It made no difference to the bounty hunter.

He automatically rammed the cigarillo between his sharp teeth and struck a match as the palomino stallion continued to walk to where it could smell water. Iron Eyes inhaled the smoke and looked ahead at the town.

He tossed the spent match aside and drew the smoke deep into his lungs. For a brief moment it eased the pain that tortured his long form.

Iron Eyes glared through the moonlight at Twin Forks.

A large livery stable stood at the edge of the town. A glowing light danced across its open doors. The bounty hunter tilted his head as his long-legged mount walked past it. The sight of the blacksmith's forge deep inside the structure caught his attention. For some unknown reason Iron Eyes thought about Squirrel Sally and the battered old stagecoach she used to dog his trail. She was so much like him, he thought. She was incapable of quitting when she had the scent of her prey in her tiny nose. The trouble was that for some reason he still could not fathom, she hunted him. Squirrel Sally was besotted with him and that made no sense at all in his mind.

A dog barked. The stallion shied for an instant.

His mind then returned to the town that faced him. Iron Eyes narrowed his piercing stare at the moonlit town. The streets were lit up as were many of the buildings, but there was something not quite right.

Something began to gnaw at his innards.

Iron Eyes dropped his left hand. It disappeared into the trail-coat pocket. His fingers curled around his Navy Colt's grip and trigger. He was still a few minutes away from the centre of town but his ever keen instincts kept telling him that something was definitely wrong.

The brightly illuminated settlement was different from the way it usually was. At first the injured horseman could not think what was wrong; then it dawned on him.

His blood-starved eyes focused as best they could on what was before him. They darted from one building to the next in search of people. There was not one living soul to be seen out on the streets. None at all and that was totally out of character for the usually bustling border town.

The streets being empty surprised the deadly bounty hunter. In all the times he had ventured to this remote town he had never before seen it so devoid of humanity. It troubled Iron Eyes as the stallion walked towards a moonlit marker.

He eased back on his reins and stared down at the crude wooden marker, which looked like a tombstone. Iron Eyes sighed and read the words burned into its wooden surface.

'Twin Forks. Population 420,' Iron Eyes said aloud as though trying to convince his aching head that he had reached the right place. He sucked hard on his cigar in a vain attempt to forget the pain which tormented him.

It seemed impossible that not one of over 400 people would be out in the moonlit streets.

'Where the hell are they?' Iron Eyes wondered as his hand caressed the gun in his pocket.

There were many reasons why a town like Twin Forks might have fallen virtually silent, he reasoned. Yet the only one that satisfied the horseman was that it had something to do with Joe Hyams and Buster Jones.

He knew they had a reputation for being more than willing to kill anyone who happened to look at them the wrong way, but were they capable of scaring an entire town into hiding?

Maybe the smarter of the towns-people knew that trouble was coming and they wanted no part of it.

A cruel smile carved its way across his hideous features.

'Be afraid,' Iron Eyes whispered through cigar smoke. 'Be real afraid. Nobody bushwhacks me and lives to brag about it.'

The gruesome rider tapped his spurs. The powerful palomino walked slowly on into the outskirts of Twin Forks. He could hear the sound of people's voices coming from two of the saloons set in the centre of the town. Again his eyes darted from one side of the main street to the other. Not only were the stores shuttered but every one of the settlement's saloons was also locked up tight. That in itself was something Iron Eyes had never seen before.

He guided the horse deeper into the town with the finger and thumb of his right hand. With each step of the palomino's long legs the horseman's eyes moved from behind the strands of his limp hair.

Iron Eyes pulled the gun from his pocket. His thumb eased its hammer back until it fully locked into position. He kept searching the shadows for any sign of the two outlaws he hunted.

Although the bounty hunter would never have admitted it, he was deeply troubled by the fact that apart from saddle horses tied at various hitching rails, there was no sign of life. Like all the towns that stretched along the border Twin Forks usually slept during the day and only came to life after sundown.

His cold eyes continued vainly to search for those he hunted. Others had marked them for death and he was merely their executioner. Usually Iron Eyes had no feelings towards those he was about to kill, but the throbbing of the savage wound on the side of his head kept reminding him that now it was personal.

The powerful palomino responded to its master as the sharp spurs tapped and guided it out from the shadows and into the bright moonlight. As he rode down the middle of the wide street Iron Eyes knew that he was again a target just as he had been out on the prairie.

Yet Iron Eyes was unafraid. The fear of dying only frightened those he considered cowards.

He defied his enemy's bullets to seek him out for a second time. The thought that he might die he allowed never to enter his mind for to do so was to admit the possibility that he, like them, was mortal and that did not sit well in his hunter's soul.

He rested his Navy Colt on his saddle horn as his prized stallion continued to walk slowly down the street. This time he was ready. One noise or even an unexpected shadow would draw his lethal lead.

Iron Eyes had no intention of being shot again.

There were a score of horses at various hitching poles along the winding street. By their appearance most of them seemed to have been there for a long while. They silently endured the cold night air, waiting for their masters' return.

Then as the palomino drew close to one of the saloons, which was still open for business, Iron Eyes noticed two horses which were in total contrast to all of the others. The lantern light fell upon both horse and rider as the bounty hunter eased back on his reins.

Iron Eyes turned the stallion full circle as he coldly studied both the saddle horses. There were so many horses dotted along the main street of

Twin Forks but only two that were covered in sweat. They had been tied up between other horses at the saloon's hitching rail but to the eyes of the ruthless bounty hunter they stood out.

Steam rose from the two mounts tied up outside the Lucky Horseshoe saloon. Sweat suds covered them. It betrayed the fact that they had been ridden hard to this place and had not had time to cool down like the rest of the horses in the street.

Fire filled the eyes of the wounded Iron Eyes. He gritted his teeth and tapped his spurs.

'I reckon I've got you now, boys,' Iron Eyes said as he steered the palomino away from the saloon. The elegant palomino walked away from the Lucky Horseshoe as its master started to consider how he was going to kill the two outlaws.

The bounty hunter aimed his stallion at a water trough outside the sheriff's office. He studied the familiar building. It was shrouded in darkness but Iron

Eyes was not fooled.

He had met Sheriff Pat O'Hara before and knew it was his habit to lock himself inside his office if there was even a hint of trouble in the town he was meant to protect.

'Reckon the sheriff is keeping his head down,' Iron Eyes muttered to the obedient horse beneath him. 'Just like the last time I had call to visit the critter.'

The scent of the water in the trough drew the thirsty horse quickly across the sand towards it. The palomino stopped, dropped its head and started to drink. Iron Eyes eased himself off his mount and moved towards the small building. He looped his reins around the porch upright and tied a secure knot. His eyes darted to the horse.

'Drink your fill,' Iron Eyes told the mount. 'You earned it.'

The tall, battle-scarred figure raised his eyes for a brief moment and looked back at the saloon. They were in there, he told himself. Soon he would join them. Then they would die.

The saloon was just far enough away from the shadowy office to be out of range of most six-shooters. Without even realizing it Iron Eyes patted the neck of his powerful horse.

He stepped up on to the boardwalk and tried the door handle. It was locked, just as he knew it would be.

There was no time for niceties.

Iron Eyes still had one of his Navy Colts in his hand and thrust its long barrel through the small pane of glass nearest the lock. The glass shattered into the dark interior of the office.

Again Iron Eyes glanced around the street. There was still not one living soul anywhere to be seen. He reached inside and found the door key in the lock. He turned the key, opened the door and entered. Moonlight trailed in behind him and cast a black shadow against a far wall. It was his shadow and it looked as trail-weary as he felt.

The tall, injured bounty hunter paused.

It took a few seconds for his eyes to adjust to the dark interior of the office. Then he saw the seated figure of O'Hara in a corner with a bottle of whiskey in one hand and a cocked .44 in the other.

'Give me a good reason why I shouldn't shoot you, stranger,' the sheriff said.

Iron Eyes tilted his head. His long hair fell over his shoulder as he looked hard at the lawman. The moonlight caught his eyes as they glared across the office.

'Howdy, Sheriff.'

'Iron Eyes?' The sheriff questioned his own eyesight as he saw the deathly face of the wounded bounty hunter loom over his desk. He had seen the horrific face before but it had never looked quite as bad as it did now. Even the soft light of the moon which managed to filter through the small window behind the lawman could not disguise the hideous new wound Iron Eyes sported.

'Who else would come riding into this cesspit of a town?' Iron Eyes asked.

The lawman rose to his feet and pushed his gun back into its holster. He walked around his desk and approached the injured bounty hunter.

'What the hell happened to you?' O'Hara asked, and gulped.

Iron Eyes did not reply. He pulled the cigar from his mouth and grabbed the sheriff's bottle. He raised it to his lips, took a long swallow and then sat down on the edge of the desk. He looked as though he were ready to drop, but O'Hara knew that here was a man whom it did not pay to underestimate.

'Good grief!' O'Hara could not take his eyes off the terrible wound. 'You should be dead by the look of that wound, boy. That's a killing wound.'

Iron Eyes took another swig of the whiskey. 'I don't die that easy.'

'But what happened to you?'

'I got myself bushwhacked.' Iron Eyes shrugged. 'The two varmints I've been hunting decided to part my head in the middle. Reckon they figured I was dead, so then they carried on here.'

'How ain't you dead, boy?' the sheriff asked. He squinted at the wound and its crude, gruesome repair work. 'How did you do that?'

'I kinda melted the skin together.' Iron Eyes downed more whiskey. 'It worked. The bleeding stopped.'

'It sure is a real ugly job, boy,' O'Hara observed. 'You burned a lot of hair off your damn head as well as melting the skin together.'

Iron Eyes sighed and pointed to the wound. 'I don't give a damn how I look. I got me other things on my mind. Like killing the varmints who did this to me.'

O'Hara looked nervous.

Even more nervous than he usually appeared to be when there were outlaws within the limits of his town. He pointed a shaking finger out of the open door.

'They're over yonder in the Lucky Horseshoe.'

Iron Eyes lifted the bottle to his scarred lips and took another long swallow of the fiery liquor. The fumes invigorated him.

'I figured that already, Sheriff,' he said as he eased his long lean frame back to its full height. 'I saw their steamed-up nags outside.'

The lawman looked fearful as he stepped into the moonlight and peered up into the expressionless face. O'Hara was shaking and the savage wounds did nothing to quell his terror.

'What you gonna do, Iron Eyes?' he asked. 'What you intending to do?'

The bounty hunter paced to the open doorway and stared out at the saloon beyond his palamino drinking at the trough. He inhaled deeply and smiled. His eyes wandered back from the Lucky Horseshoe and rested upon the rotund lawman.

O'Hara fought his fear and moved closer to the hideously injured bounty hunter. He rubbed the sweat from his plump face and repeated his question.

'Damn you, Iron Eyes. Tell me. What are you intending to do?'

'Kill them,' Iron Eyes replied drily. 'What else?'

9

Not being laden down by the weight of passengers and luggage the six-horse team had made good time as it drew Squirrel Sally's stagecoach across the arid, moonlit prairie towards its goal. With every passing moment the relentless coach drew ever closer to the border town, which was now only a few miles ahead. Clouds of choking dust rose heavenwards from the horses' hoofs and the wheel rims of the speeding conveyance. The young unconscious female lay bound hand and foot inside the rocking vehicle as Wolfe guided the stage towards Twin Forks.

For a one-armed man Wolfe was more than capable of handling the well-rested team of horses. He sat up on the high driver's board and urged the galloping horses on.

Wolfe had no way of knowing it but he had narrowed the gap between himself and the bounty hunter drastically since setting out from Santa Rosa. Iron Eyes had taken far longer than he realized to recover from the savage bullet wound that had brought him to an abrupt halt in his pursuit of Hyams and Jones.

Wolfe had used that time to gain relentlessly on his unwitting prey.

The stagecoach moved smoothly along the prairie road and began its descent into a dusty draw when Wolfe spotted something a few hundred yards ahead of his lead horses. His cruel eyes narrowed as they tried to make out what it was that he had spied strewn across the otherwise pristine sand.

Even the eerie light of the bright moon could not disguise the fact that whatever was lying on the sand, it was certainly dead.

The one-armed man held on to the hefty reins, pressed a boot against the brake pole and slowed the team as the large vehicle approached the unidentified obstruction.

Wolfe locked the brake pole and looped the long leathers around it. He carefully climbed down from his lofty perch and drew his six-shooter from its holster.

Before he had taken even a step shadows fell upon the ground around him. Wolfe glanced upwards and saw a pair of black-headed vultures circling.

He gritted his teeth and walked along the length of the team with his gun held at hip level.

As he advanced away from the lead horses his eyes began to focus more clearly on the carnage before him. Wolfe halted as he reached the first of the dead coyotes.

'What the hell happened here?' Wolfe mumbled as he tried to work out why the trail was littered with dead canines. Keeping the cocked weapon in his hand he darted his gaze to the thicket of Joshua trees and high cactus. Then he returned his attention to the bodies of the dead animals.

He was about to go back to the

stagecoach when he saw the bottles close to one of the dead carcasses. Wolfe strode to the bottles and stared down at them.

Both were whiskey bottles and both were empty.

'Iron Eyes,' Wolfe said confidently. 'But why'd he kill all these critters? That bastard never wastes bullets on anything if it ain't got a price on its head.'

He holstered his gun and rubbed his unshaven jaw. None of this made any sense to the cold-hearted man. Then he noticed something that began to reveal the truth to him.

Wolfe knelt and ran his hand across the dark sand.

'Blood,' Wolfe said. He rose to his feet again. 'And it ain't belonging to these coyotes. This is his blood.'

The more Wolfe studied the ground the more blood he noticed. He then saw the deep impression in the sand where the bounty hunter had landed after being winged. It still retained his long, unmistakable shape.

'He was shot,' Wolfe noted. The one-armed man spun on his heel and ran back towards the stagecoach. Every sinew in his body knew that the man he was hunting was badly wounded and yet, even though Iron Eyes had obviously spilled more blood than most could afford to lose, he had somehow ridden on towards Twin Forks.

How?

What did it take to kill him?

The entire story was laid out on the sand and Wolfe had read it expertly. Iron Eyes had been ambushed. The bounty hunter had been badly wounded, going by the amount of blood which he had lost. Whoever had shot Iron Eyes must have imagined he had achieved his goal and killed him, otherwise he would have finished the job. The coyotes must have been drawn by the scent of fresh blood and Iron Eyes had shot them before they sank their fangs into him.

Then somehow Iron Eyes had ridden on.

For the first time since he had started

hunting the notorious Iron Eyes, Wolfe wondered what kind of man he was on the trail of. If indeed the bounty hunter *was* a man. Like so many others in the West Wolfe had heard the stories concerning the infamous bounty hunter.

The more he considered the evidence before him the more clearly the one-armed man recalled his last encounter with Iron Eyes.

A chill traced his spine.

It had nothing to do with the temperature.

It had everything to do with doubt and fear. Doubt that he might not be able to achieve the only thing that had kept him hunting the notorious bounty hunter since he had buried his arm eighteen months earlier. Fear that all the ludicrous stories he heard about Iron Eyes were actually true.

Iron Eyes was still alive yet the amount of blood he had spilled on the moonlit sand made that seem a total impossibility.

Yet it was true.

A groan came from the interior of the stagecoach. Wolfe turned his head and looked inside at the small figure of Squirrel Sally as she began to awaken.

Her eyes could see little apart from the floor of the vehicle. She inhaled the familiar scent of death, which still lingered upon its wooden decking. The feisty female was about to speak when she felt the looped rope that held her wrists together. Then, as her shapely form wriggled, she realized that her ankles were also tied together.

Then she remembered.

'Wolfe!' The name dripped from her lips like poison.

'That's right, gal,' Wolfe sneered in the moonlight.

Her beautiful eyes darted up and saw his face glaring down at her. She was confused.

'Let me go,' Sally insisted.

'Not yet,' Wolfe said in a chilling voice. 'You're a hunter just like that monster I'm tracking. You gotta know it don't pay to release your bait until you've trapped the critter you're hunting. Right?'

'All I gotta do is scream and half Santa Rosa will swarm all over you, Wolfe,' she replied.

Wolfe smiled. 'That would be right if we was still in Santa Rosa, gal. We ain't. We're spitting distance from Twin Forks.'

'What?' Squirrel Sally somehow managed to clamber up on to her knees. She stared out at the arid prairie bathed in the bluish hue of the bright moon. Her heart raced as she fell back on to her rump. 'What's going on?'

Wolfe did not answer. He climbed back up the side of the stagecoach to the driver's seat and freed the reins from the brake pole. His smile evaporated. He sighed heavily as he recalled the pain he had suffered when his arm had been nearly severed by the accurate bullets with which Iron Eyes had shot him. He raised his leg and aimed his boot heel at the metal lock, which held in place. Wolfe kicked the lock off the brake pole and it sprang back towards him.

He lashed the long leathers down across the backs of the six-horse team and steered them round the obstacles. As the large rear wheel of the stage cleared the last of the dead coyotes the one-armed man gave out a chilling yell.

The team of horses responded and gathered pace.

Wolfe ignored the furious curses which were coming from inside the coach. Squirrel Sally could rant all she liked. It would not change a thing. Wolfe knew that there was only one hope of getting the better of the strange creature known as Iron Eyes.

The little female he now held prisoner was the only weakness in the devilish bounty hunter's armour. Wolfe had to exploit that and use her to destroy the man who had destroyed his once unblemished career as a hired gun.

Iron Eyes might have nine lives but Squirrel Sally only had one and the gaunt scarecrow knew it. Wolfe was certain that the bounty hunter would never allow her to pay for his sins. She was the bait on his hook.

'Keep screaming, Sally,' Wolfe growled. 'You're doing me a darn favour and you don't even know it.'

As the stagecoach travelled through the forest with its thorny undergrowth, and rocked back and forth on the sandy road towards the lights of Twin Forks, one question kept gnawing at Wolfe's craw.

How could anyone lose that much blood and still be alive?

Why wasn't Iron Eyes already dead?

Another question festered inside Wolfe's mind.

Even if Squirrel Sally's howling did draw Iron Eyes from cover and he managed to get him in the sights of his six-shooter, would his bullets be able to kill him when so many others had failed?

The stagecoach thundered on.

10

There seemed to be little evidence of life in either the brutalized face or the body of the tall, emaciated bounty hunter as he leaned against the doorframe and stared out at the continuing revelry in the Lucky Horseshoe. If there was any colour left in his flesh it didn't show in the eerie light of the moon. He looked little better than any of the bodies down at the funeral parlour; sheer hatred and unyielding willpower kept his tall, thin frame standing upright. Iron Eyes was an unholy sight and O'Hara could not understand how anyone with such a savage wound could have survived, let alone ride miles until he reached the border town seeking vengeance.

The lawman felt genuine concern. He seemed to be expecting the stubborn bounty hunter to collapse at any moment, like a felled tree, but Iron Eyes refused to succumb to his injuries however severe they were.

'You got any more whiskey, Sheriff?' Iron Eyes asked through cigar smoke as his unblinking eyes continued to burn across the wide street.

'It ain't whiskey you need, boy,' O'Hara said. 'You need grub and doctoring.'

Iron Eyes diverted his attention to the rotund figure beside him. He drew in smoke and blew a long line of it down at the shorter man.

'Is that a yes or a no?'

The lawman shook his head. He walked to his desk, opened a drawer and pulled out a full bottle of the amber liquor. He handed it to the expressionless bounty hunter.

'Here,' O'Hara snorted. 'I don't see that it's very smart to get drunk and then go hunting.'

Iron Eyes extracted the cork with his teeth and spat it out into the street. His bony left hand raised the bottle until its neck was at his lips. He swallowed more than a quarter of its contents, then lowered it back down.

'I'd agree with you if I was a man who could get drunk, Sheriff,' the bounty hunter replied in a whisper. 'Truth of the matter is I've never been able to get drunk. This stuff just kills the pain and burns the trail dust down my throat.'

O'Hara shook his head. 'I feel sorry for you. Getting fall-down drunk is all some folks have to look forward to.'

Iron Eyes pulled his guns from his weather-proof coat and poked them behind his belt buckle. He sighed and rested the palm of his hand against the terrible gash on the side of his head.

The war drums continued to pound inside his skull.

'You want a scattergun to go with them Navy Colts, Iron Eyes?' the sheriff asked.

Iron Eyes shook his head.

'Nope. Scatterguns tend to kill too fast. I intend making them boys die real slow, Sheriff.' The bounty hunter sucked more smoke into his lungs and gripped the cigar with his teeth.

O'Hara exhaled nervously. 'Listen up. Why don't you just go to see old Doc Parry, boy? Get that wound fixed properly. Them boys will still be there in the morning and a whole lot easier to catch.'

The bounty hunter turned and stared down at the shorter man. His thin left hand pulled the two Wanted posters from his pocket and unfolded them.

'Read that,' Iron Eyes snarled and pointed at the three words printed on each of the posters.

'Dead or alive,' the sheriff said.

'Exactly. I don't intend catching them stinking critters, Sheriff,' Iron Eyes said. He rammed both the posters back into his pocket next to the loose bullets. 'I intend killing them damn slow.'

The lawman passed a hand across his sweat-soaked neck and then rubbed it down his shirt front. 'There are innocent folks in that saloon, boy. I don't want you killing no innocent folks. Do you hear me? Do you?'

'A deaf man could hear you,' Iron Eyes replied.

'I mean it,' O'Hara emphasized. 'I don't want to see innocent people getting killed. Do you savvy?'

Iron Eyes shrugged. 'I savvy real fine, Sheriff. Now maybe you oughta go and tell Hyams and Buster the same thing. I reckon that if anyone gets in between me and them they sure better duck real fast. Those boys tend to kill anything they see.'

O'Hara defied his own fear and stood toe to toe with the brutal bounty hunter.

'And what about you, Iron Eyes? Do you kill anything you see?' the lawman asked.

Iron Eyes handed the bottle to the sheriff and stepped out on to the boardwalk. His horse was still drinking from the trough as he glanced over his wide shoulder back at the lawman's face.

'I never waste bullets on folks that ain't got bounty on their heads, Sheriff.'

Iron Eyes stepped down on to the sand and walked to the cream-coloured rump of his mount. 'Feed my horse. You'll find grain in my bags.'

Before O'Hara could respond Iron Eyes had vanished like a phantom into the shadows. The lawman stepped out and walked over to the horse. His squinting eyes searched in vain for the tall, blood-soaked figure.

Then he heard the haunting sound of spurs ringing out in the quiet street. A cold chill made O'Hara shiver. It was as if someone had just walked across his grave. His shaking hands lifted the flap of the nearest saddlebag satchel and found a bag of grain.

He pulled it out and cradled it in his arms. He then moved to the head of the magnificent palomino stallion, leaned over and poured some of the grain on to the sand.

When he straightened up he suddenly saw the image of the tall, thin bounty hunter walking into the lantern light further down the street.

Sheriff O'Hara could feel his heart pounding underneath his shirt. He tried to swallow but there was no spittle. The lawman returned the bag of grain to the saddlebags and then ran back to his office.

He paused by the open doorway.

The lawman watched as Iron Eyes headed towards the saloon with both guns in his skeletal hands.

The sheriff rushed into his office, slammed its door and turned the key. He plucked up the whiskey bottle and raised it to his mouth. He started to drink feverishly.

Unlike the bounty hunter, O'Hara could get drunk.

He intended to do so.

11

The almost orange light of the lanterns spread out from the saloon and nearly reached the far side of the wide street. It illuminated the horses at the hitching rail and the thin, blood-covered figure who strode towards the boisterous Lucky Horseshoe with his Navy Colts gripped in his hands.

The noise from inside the saloon was in complete contrast to the quiet in the rest of the town. The closer Iron Eyes got to the swing doors the louder it got. The bounty hunter had heard similar noises from countless other saloons in his time. A cocktail of female and male voices mixed with a badly tuned piano washed over the unblinking Iron Eyes as he walked around the tethered horses and stepped up on to the boardwalk.

He paused. The two horses with

steam rising from them were still there. Still waiting for their masters to emerge from the saloon. Stained in dried blood the awesome figure of Iron Eyes walked like a vengeful ghost towards the front of the saloon. He did not stop until he had reached the swing doors and rested the barrels of his Navy Colts upon them. His eyes burned into the lantern-lit saloon. It was busier than he had imagined and was filled with scores of people who had no idea what was about to happen once he had entered.

Iron Eyes stared over the swing doors and searched for the two faces whose images he had on the folded Wanted posters buried deep in his trail-coat pocket.

He was like an eagle high on a thermal, seeking out its prey. He would not stop his hunt until he had claimed the lives of the two wanted men. Nothing but death itself could stop him.

It no longer had anything to do with the price on Joe Hyams's and Buster Jones's heads. The severely wounded bounty hunter would willingly have killed both outlaws for free.

The smell of sweat mingled with that of tobacco smoke and stale liquor. It filled the nostrils of the deadly onlooker as he lowered his head and focused through the long limp locks of matted hair that hung before his icy glare.

The tobacco smoke masked the staircase at the far end of the saloon from even the sharpest of eyes. Iron Eyes noted the lanterns and chandelier whose light bathed the interior of the Lucky Horseshoe in unforgiving brightness. He didn't like that much light because it sometimes allowed those he was hunting to see him before he had spotted them.

His thumbs cocked the hammers of his guns until they fully locked. The sound of the Navy Colts being readied for action drew the attention of those closest to the swing doors. A hundred eyes darted towards the gruesome figure of Iron Eyes.

Every one of those who saw his

battle-scarred face as it peered into the Lucky Horseshoe seemed to gasp in horror at exactly the same moment.

Scores of people moved away from the terrifying apparition. Suddenly the sound of talking and laughter turned to screams. Iron Eyes knew there was no more time to think. Now he had to act whilst he still had the strength to do so.

Few men would have considered entering a place where there were so many gun grips protruding from so many holsters but Iron Eyes knew that the men he sought were somewhere within its crowded confines.

With each beat of his labouring heart he knew that the chances of his surviving were becoming less certain. He gritted his teeth and narrowed his eyes and walked forward through the obliging swing doors.

His bloodstained mule-eared boots stopped a few paces into the saloon. He listened to the doors rocking on their hinges behind his broad back and continued his search for the outlaws who, he sensed, were now closer than they had ever been to the bullets in his guns. Bar-room girls clambered over the tables and tried to hide, but there was nowhere to go except up against the wooden walls of the Lucky Horseshoe. Gamblers had scattered along with their drunken victims but they too found that there was no sanctuary. A hundred or more people pressed up against all three walls that faced the tall, emaciated figure as Iron Eyes held his guns at hip height and his cold eyes continued to search out his prey.

Then one of the men pulled his .45 from its holster and charged towards the impassive figure. The youngster was either a wanted outlaw who had recognized the legendary bounty hunter or he was just so scared that he had lost his sanity. Either way he started to fan his gun hammer.

Three bullets cut through the stale bar-room air and passed within inches of the unmoving Iron Eyes. The tall man did not move a muscle apart from those in his arms and hands. He jerked both his guns towards the running gunman and squeezed their triggers.

Deafening fury hit the young gunman dead centre and lifted him off his feet. With the smoking gun still in his hand the foolhardy youngster flew backwards and crashed heavily into the sawdust.

Iron Eyes strode to the body and looked down at his deadly handiwork. He spat at the face he did not recognize. This was neither of the outlaws he was hunting, he thought. He swung around on his heels. Smoke trailed from his gun barrels.

'Damn it all!' he cursed, and his eyes returned to those who were pressed up against the walls. 'Where the hell are Hyams and Jones?'

There was not a single reply.

These terrified people trapped inside the saloon either did not know the answer to his simple question or they were just too afraid to speak.

The cigar- and pipe-smoke hung at Stetson height across the room. It swirled around the interior of the room like ghostly whirlpools in the air as Iron Eyes ventured towards the long bar counter set beneath the carpeted staircase. His eyes darted around the men and women as they huddled together against the walls. Then he heard sobbing as some of the females caught sight of his tortured features.

With each stride of his long, thin legs the sound of his spurs tolled their fateful melody.

There was a new smell inside the saloon.

It was the scent of fear.

Iron Eyes was within ten feet of the bar and the shaking bartender when he heard the floorboards on the landing above him creak.

'You looking for us?' a voice boomed out from the top of the staircase.

The bounty hunter paused, squinted up through the tobacco smoke and saw two half-dressed men. Iron Eyes did not say a word as his eyes burned across the distance between them and focused on their faces. The very same faces that were printed on the Wanted posters in his deep trail-coat pocket.

It was Hyams who recognized the horrendous creature first.

'Iron Eyes?' he blurted as his partner dragged his Colt from its holster. Their blood chilled in their veins as they looked down on the figure who was bathed from head to boot in his own gore.

'We killed you. You're dead,' Buster Jones yelled down.

Hyams glanced at Jones. 'We shot him in the head. He can't still be alive.'

Jones screamed down angrily from the landing and waved his gun at the defiant bounty hunter, who was standing watching them with unblinking determination.

'You're dead.'

A shocked gasp swept around the saloon.

Iron Eyes dragged his gun hammers back again and gritted his teeth. He ignored the agony that tortured his skeletal body, and stretched himself up to his full height.

'If that's so then I reckon you're gonna be killed by a dead man,' he snarled.

12

At the very same moment that the stage-coach came to an abrupt halt in the middle of the long main street, all hell broke loose inside the Lucky Horse-shoe. The entire town shook as guns inside the saloon exploded into action. Shafts of light beamed out of bullet holes which peppered the walls and roof of the weather-worn building. Wolfe had kicked the brake pole so suddenly that the two lead horses became tangled in their traces and crashed violently into the sand. The four following horses of the team did what all horses try to do when faced with something directly in their path. They vainly attempted to avoid the fallen horses. But their chains prevented any escape from the inevitable. They piled up in horrifying disarray.

The unyielding trio of wooden guide poles that were set between the horses arched. One snapped like matchwood, sending countless splinters into the flesh of the stricken horses. The entire stagecoach was lifted sideways off the ground. On one side its wheels spun in the air, then the entire stagecoach toppled over and landed on its side. A fraction of a second before the body of the coach hit the sand Wolfe leapt clear.

The one-armed man rolled over and over and ended up on his knees next to a trough. He brushed the sand from his face and listened to the shooting.

Wolfe had barely noticed the mishap that had sent him cartwheeling from his lofty perch.

All he could do was think about the saloon a few hundred yards ahead of him. There was a battle to end all battles going on inside the Lucky Horseshoe. That meant only one thing to the man with only one arm. It meant he had finally caught up with the bounty hunter he had hunted for so long.

'So that's where you are, Iron Eyes,' Wolfe grunted like a man who has just discovered a gold nugget. He staggered to his feet, then noticed the glint of a tin star to his left. Wolfe turned and saw Sheriff O'Hara move across the sand towards the stricken stagecoach.

Even a lawman who had always tried to avoid conflict could not ignore the unholy sound of the war which was being waged inside the Lucky Horseshoe. When he had also seen the stagecoach crashing not a hundred feet from his office, O'Hara had found himself drawn out into the street.

He was like a moth being lured towards a lantern's light.

Every instinct he had honed over a lifetime was forgotten as the rotund figure rushed to where the stagecoach lay on its side. Something he had thought was buried deep inside him had suddenly been rekindled.

It was the very reason he had first chosen to pin on a tin star so many years before. The sheriff wanted to help anyone who might require his assistance.

Wolfe stared through the lantern light

148

at the lawman. His hand found the gun in its hand-tooled holster. He flicked the small leather safety loop of its hammer. His eyes burned at the lawman.

'Are you OK, stranger?' O'Hara shouted at Wolfe.

Wolfe did not reply, but slowly approached the stagecoach.

'I'll check your passengers,' the sheriff shouted.

'Ain't got no passengers,' Wolfe shouted back.

O'Hara looked at the vehicle on its side. He began to realize that it did not belong to either of the stagecoach companies that regularly visited Twin Forks.

'What's going on here?' the lawman asked as he studied the man with only one arm standing before him. 'This ain't one of the regular stages. Who are you?'

Before Wolfe could say anything Squirrel Sally mustered all her strength and called out for help from inside the coach. Wolfe's finger eased in around his gun trigger.

'Help me,' Sally groaned pitifully from deep inside the upturned stagecoach.

'No passengers, huh?' The sheriff frowned. 'That's a gal's voice in there.'

With deafening shots still ringing out from the saloon, the fat sheriff moved faster than he had managed to do in more than ten years and climbed up on to the stricken coach. He looked into its dark interior and saw the petite female lying below him. He pulled the door open and reached down.

'Take my hand, young 'un,' O'Hara said. Then he noticed that Squirrel Sally could not move. Her ankles and wrists were hogtied. 'What's going on here?'

Just as O'Hara looked up and across the moonlit street at Wolfe he saw the flash from the gun in the one-armed man's hand.

The sheriff felt the impact of the bullet and fell back off the top of the coach. He hit the sand hard.

Wolfe marched back to the coach and fired another shot into the lawman. Then he holstered his gun and climbed up the wooden vehicle and sat on it. He could see his captive below him. She was bruised and bloodied but there was still fire in her large eyes.

'I'd best get the bait out,' Wolfe drawled.

13

Frenzied shots continued splintering through the timber walls of the saloon. The deafening rat-a-tat of gunfire mixed with the raised voices in the smoke-filled saloon. Now tobacco smoke was secondary to the continuous plumes of gunsmoke which trailed from the six-shooters of the three determined gunmen. Angry shouts were soon overwhelmed by the pathetic screams of terrified customers.

The Lucky Horseshoe was littered with the bodies of the innocent as the pair of hardy outlaws kept their weaponry firing down into the heart of the saloon.

Iron Eyes used the dead as cover while his thin fingers reloaded his guns with the loose ammunition he always kept in his deep trail-coat pockets. The haze of gunsmoke made it virtually impossible to see the pair of deadly outlaws above him on the landing.

Only the red flashes of their guns as fingers teased triggers gave any clue as to where the pair of outlaws were from one moment to the next. Hyams and Jones knew they had to keep moving if they were to avoid the fate so many of their profession had suffered over the years. To stand still for too long was to allow the deadly hunter's marksmanship to find his targets.

The sudden eruption of gunfire in the saloon's bar had taken all the customers by surprise. Panic now gripped those who were still alive. The wounded desperately tried to crawl away from the incessant gunfire whilst the dead were piled up for cover by the bounty hunter.

Iron Eyes unleashed another volley of lead at the landing high above him, then ran to the edge of the long bar counter.

He watched without emotion as bullets tore up the bodies he had just been sheltering behind. He poked one gun into his belt and shook the spent casings from his hot gun. The two men kept firing down from various points on the landing as Iron Eyes pushed fresh bullets into the smoking weapon.

'I must be getting old,' he whispered to himself. He snapped the Navy Colt together and hauled its hammer back into position again. 'This used to be a whole lot easier.'

Just like startled steers most of the people trapped against the walls stampeded. An almost blind panic swept through them. Then, as even more of the innocents were hit by the random bullets of the outlaws, they sought refuge behind tables. Self-preservation was a powerful instinct often not controlled by reason. On numerous occasions lives had been lost when a mass of people attempted to flee at the very same moment.

The groans of the wounded could be heard all around the saloon.

Iron Eyes did not like the sound. He always tried to kill the creatures he hunted clean.

The bartender was crouched down behind the mahogany bar counter. His eyes widened when he saw Iron Eyes appear around the corner of it. Then the screams grew even louder as half a dozen shots shattered a wall lantern. The burning oil covered the papered wooden wall in flames.

Fire rose up through the tinder-dry woodwork of the saloon and enveloped the exposed rafters. The entire town rocked with the ceaseless racket of gunplay. Those females who had not been cut down by the crossfire of bullets staggered out into the street. Some were wounded and the fancy dresses of others were aflame. All were possessed of one desire: they wanted to escape and survive.

The people of the town who had been drawn first to the noise and then to the fire tried to fight the flames with water from the many troughs scattered along the main street.

The majority simply watched in mindless awe.

Only those who had been inside the two-storey building knew exactly what had happened to start the mayhem and most of them would never be able to tell the tale. As smoke billowed out from the wide-open doorway and windows the shooting continued within the blazing inferno. The sound of raised, angry voices had ceased but the screams still echoed out into the small border town.

Screams of fear had become screams of pain.

The tall, emaciated figure looked around the long room as the growing light of the fire illuminated the carnage. Iron Eyes grabbed the arm of the bartender and hauled him to his feet.

'Run,' Iron Eyes told him.

Few sane men ever argued with the tall bounty hunter. One glance at his scarred features was enough to tell anyone that this creature was unlike all other men. He wore the wounds of every fight and battle he had endured on his face.

The bartender leapt over the counter and kept running through the smoke and flames. The ghostlike figure walked the distance to where a whiskey bottle stood next to a freckled mirror. He pulled its cork, raised the clear glass neck to his lips and drank.

Between each gulp he surveyed the room. The bartender had made it to the swing doors and had disappeared out into the moonlight. The bodies of those who had not been so fortunate lay in the sawdust on the floor.

The fire had spread across the dry rafters and now reached the opposite side of the saloon. Burning paint dripped down its walls, igniting everything in its path.

Iron Eyes placed the bottle down and looked up to where he could see bullets from the outlaws' guns cutting scarlet traces through the smoke.

Faster than the blink of an eye Iron Eyes fanned his gun hammer and aimed his Colt to either side of the telltale rods of deadly lead.

He heard a yelp.

He had winged one of the men he hunted.

The jingling of the loose bullets buried deep in his trail-coat pockets echoed around the saloon with every stride as Iron Eyes made his way towards the foot of the staircase. A flight of steps which were already alight might have seemed insurmountable to most men but not the bounty hunter. He knew that every avenue of escape from the ground floor was now closed to him. He had to get up to the landing where the outlaws were if he were to find a way out of the blazing saloon.

The long black mane of hair floated on his shoulders as Iron Eyes swung up and over the handrail. The sound of his vicious spurs rang out as he landed a quarter of the way up the staircase.

Hyams was holding his left arm as blood spread between his fingers. He edged behind his partner.

'We gotta get out of this place before we end up like a pair of Thanksgiving turkeys, Buster.'

Buster Jones nodded. He had heard the sound of the spurs on the staircase and knew that only a madman would hang around to see the hideous bounty hunter emerge from the flames and smoke.

'We can jump out through the back window, Joe,' Jones suggested.

'Yeah, if that ain't on fire like the rest of this damn saloon,' Hyams agreed. Both men fumbled their way through the smoke towards the corridor which led to the rear of the Lucky Horseshoe. They knew that they would have to drop twenty feet down to the ground but that was a whole lot better than getting roasted alive.

The flames licked up the walls inside the saloon as Iron Eyes mounted the staircase. He reached the landing and fell on to his belly. He looked beneath the layer of choking smoke and saw the boots of the two outlaws as they sped along the corridor. Without a second's hesitation Iron Eyes fanned the hammer of his Navy Colt.

The scream told him that he had hit one of them.

It did not matter to Iron Eyes which of the outlaws he had winged. All that mattered was that he had again drawn blood.

The sound of the two men fearfully running down the corridor filled the saloon as Iron Eyes got to his feet and staggered forward. He reached the corner as two bullets came through the smoke and ripped the wall apart. The bounty hunter was showered in burning splinters but he did not pause for a second as flames raced across the ceiling above his head.

The corridor was filled with smoke but Iron Eyes heard the sash window being raised straight ahead of him.

Even though he could not see his prey the deadly hunter knew where they were. He fanned his gun hammer as his long lean legs strode along the corridor. Cold air greeted him as he reached the far wall and the open window. He stared at the droplets of blood on the windowsill. A cruel smile was etched upon his tortured face as he looked down into darkness. Flickering light from the flames of the burning roof danced on the sand below him.

His icy stare could see where the outlaws had landed. He dropped from the high window on to the disturbed sand, then slowly straightened up.

The soft ground told him everything he wanted to know.

Even a blind man could have followed their desperate boot prints in the otherwise undisturbed sand. They led around the side of the blazing saloon.

Iron Eyes walked and stared along the side of the building as smouldering ash rained down on the alley. Even as flames broke through the disintegrating side wall the tall figure trailed the men he sought.

There were no more sounds of screaming coming from the saloon over his shoulder, only the unmistakable noise of burning embers and exploding bottles of whiskey and tequila. The air was full of red embers and swirling smoke when Iron Eyes reached the front of the blazing building.

He paused as a bullet passed his face, and looked up at the two outlaws who had only just managed to mount their horses.

There was not a hint of expression in the scarred face of Iron Eyes as he fanned his gun hammer until the weapon was empty. He saw both the wanted men buckle as his bullets tore through them.

He rammed the smoking gun into his pocket and watched both the outlaws fall from their mounts.

Iron Eyes walked towards the survivors of the brutally brief battle and looked down at the dead men. He gave a long sigh. Then he pulled a cigar from his pocket. He was about to light it when something a hundred yards away caught his attention.

The sight confused and surprised the long lean man. Chewing on the cigar between his teeth he strode towards the troubling apparition.

With her wrists and ankles securely tied, Squirrel Sally knelt on the sand with a cocked gun at her head. The closer Iron Eyes got to the unexpected sight the more he could see.

He stopped twenty feet from the small female and the one-armed man who held the barrel of his pistol at her temple. The bounty hunter spat the cigar from his mouth.

'Wolfe,' he said in a low growl.

The one-armed man gave a nod of his head. 'Drop your hoglegs, Iron Eyes. Drop them or I'll blow her head clean off.'

Sally looked up at the man she adored. 'Don't you go listening to this critter, Iron Eyes. He ain't got the guts to face you down man to man.'

Iron Eyes pulled the gun from behind his belt buckle and dropped it on to the sand at his feet.

'And the other one,' Wolfe ordered.

The bounty hunter reached down

into his pocket and lifted the Navy Colt with finger and thumb from its depths. He dropped it beside its twin.

'Are you happy now?' Iron Eyes asked.

Wolfe glared at Iron Eyes.

'And the Bowie knife in your boot.'

'You got a good memory.' Iron Eyes shrugged and reached down to the neck of his boot. He pulled the huge knife out of its resting place and tossed it aside.

'You damn fool,' Sally screamed at the tall bounty hunter as tears filled her eyes. 'He'll still kill us both. Why'd you listen to this yella bastard?'

'He got a gun at your head, Squirrel,' Iron Eyes said.

She sobbed.

Iron Eyes tilted his head back and listened to the war drums that continued to pound inside his head. Then he saw the one-armed man take the gun away from Sally's golden hair and aim it straight at him. A sense of relief overwhelmed the bounty hunter.

Wolfe walked slowly towards the fearsome figure.

With each step he raised the barrel of his weapon. Wolfe did not stop his advance until he had the gun pressed into the bony chest of the mythic bounty hunter.

Their eyes met.

'Are you afraid, Iron Eyes?' Wolfe asked.

The bounty hunter did not utter a word. He just stared down at the vengeful face of the man he recognized. Iron Eyes knew that there was no point in trying to dissuade Wolfe from killing him.

'Say your prayers,' Wolfe snarled.

'Reckon there ain't much point,' Iron Eyes responded with a snort.

The street echoed with the unmistakable sound of a gun being fired. Squirrel Sally's head jerked up abruptly. She saw the plume of blood and watched as a figure crashed into the sand.

'No!' she cried.

Finale

The acrid smoke trailed through the lantern light across the main street from the barrel of the wounded sheriff's .44. O'Hara staggered from the shadows towards the body on the sand and looked down at his lethal handiwork. He felt no satisfaction.

'Good shot,' praised Iron Eyes.

O'Hara holstered his smoking weapon. 'That's the first time I ever shot anyone, boy.'

Iron Eyes rubbed his jaw. 'Then I figure I'm real lucky you didn't hit me instead.'

'How do you live with killing folks for a living, boy?' the lawman asked.

'It's easy.' Iron Eyes could see people heading towards the wounded sheriff. 'You get yourself off to the doc, old-timer.'

The bounty hunter scooped up his guns and knife and strode over to the sobbing female as the townspeople flocked around their sheriff.

When he reached Sally, Iron Eyes leaned over and slid the honed blade of his knife across her restraints. The rope severed and released Sally.

Sally rolled on to her bottom and looked up at the gaunt face of the man who, she thought, had only seconds before been killed by Wolfe. She wanted to smile but could not stop the tears from rolling down her cheeks.

'You're alive,' Sally gushed before noticing the horrendous new scar across the side of the bounty hunter's head.

'Disappointed?' Iron Eyes thrust his guns into his pockets and reached down.

The tiny female accepted his hand and stood up. Her fingers went to touch the brutal wound but Iron Eyes stretched up to his full height and turned away from her.

'What the hell happened to you?' Sally asked.

He raised a scarred eyebrow. 'Got myself shot again. Ain't it obvious?'

'It sure looks real bad,' Sally said.

Iron Eyes turned away from her and walked towards her crippled stagecoach. His long legs covered the ground quickly.

She trailed him to the vehicle and the still entangled team of horses which were struggling on the ground. Sally stopped beside him and vainly tried to take hold of his hand. Iron Eyes inhaled deeply and patted his trail coat until he found a cigar. He pushed it between his lips, struck a match with a thumbnail and raised it to the end of the twisted weed.

He sucked in smoke.

'What happened to you, Squirrel?' he asked curiously. 'I left you back at Santa Rosa to rest up these nags and buy some new clothes. How in tarnation did you end up here with Wolfe holding a gun at your little head?'

She stood in front of him and looked up. Her eyes were sore from the tears they had shed.

'Why'd you drop your guns and

knife?' she asked, her fingers toying with his blood-soaked shirt front. 'You could have drawn them guns and killed Wolfe before he squeezed his trigger.'

Iron Eyes inhaled more smoke, then pushed his cigar into her open mouth in a futile bid to end their embarrassing conversation.

'Hush up,' he said.

Sally took a drag on the cigar, then shook her head as she sensed something. 'Did you figure he'd kill me if you didn't do as he said?'

'Maybe,' Iron Eyes answered.

'Does that mean you actually care about me?' Sally could not stop smiling. 'Were you feared he'd kill me, Iron Eyes? Were you?'

The bounty hunter did not reply.

She reached up to return the cigar to his lips. Iron Eyes leaned down and opened his mouth. Sally jumped up and wrapped her arms around his neck. She kissed him until he managed to shake free.

There was a stunned expression on his face. She had never seen it before and it amused her. She started to giggle as he turned away and walked to where he had left his horse. Sally had to run to keep up with his long strides. Her hands tugged on his coat tails.

'Say something, Iron Eyes,' she teased. 'Tell me I'm right and you do care for me. Go on. Say something.'

Iron Eyes stopped, swung around and looked down at the petite female. He sniffed.

'You smell funny,' he drawled.

Her expression changed. 'What?'

'I said you smell funny,' he repeated.

'That's perfumed soap from a bath I had back at Santa Rosa.' She laughed and puffed on the cigar again. 'Do you like it?'

Iron Eyes grabbed the cigar from her lips and rammed it back into his own mouth. He puffed like a locomotive trying to climb a steep gradient.

'Nope, I do not. You smell like a funeral wreath.'

Sally was dancing around the towering man as if he were a totem pole. Her

170

laughter filled his head and somehow managed to drown out the war drums that had taunted him since he had been shot.

'Did you like the way I tasted, Iron Eyes?' Sally was rocking with amusement as once again the bounty hunter started walking towards the palomino stallion.

The tall man reached his horse and rested his back against the saddle. He closed his eyes thoughtfully.

She plunged a hand into his pants pocket. It drew his full attention. He gazed through the cigar smoke at her smiling face.

To Sally's total surprise he wrapped his arms around her and pulled her close. She felt safe. He did not answer her question. There was no need.

We do hope that you have enjoyed reading this large print book.

Did you know that all of our titles are available for purchase?

We publish a wide range of high quality large print books including:
Romances, Mysteries, Classics
General Fiction
Non Fiction and Westerns

Special interest titles available in large print are:
The Little Oxford Dictionary
Music Book, Song Book
Hymn Book, Service Book

Also available from us courtesy of Oxford University Press:
Young Readers' Dictionary
(large print edition)
Young Readers' Thesaurus
(large print edition)

For further information or a free brochure, please contact us at:
Ulverscroft Large Print Books Ltd.,
The Green, Bradgate Road, Anstey,
Leicester, LE7 7FU, England.
Tel: (00 44) **0116 236 4325**
Fax: (00 44) **0116 234 0205**

Other titles in the
Linford Western Library:

SPARROW'S GUN

Abe Dancer

Before setting off in pursuit of his father's murderers, Will Sparrow must learn how to handle a gun . . . Miles away from home, he plans his reprisal while working as a stable-boy. But then Laurel Wale happens along, and Will discovers his intentions aren't quite as clear-cut as he thought . . . Meanwhile, his mother has settled down nearby with one of the territory's most important citizens. She wants nothing more than peace — but nothing is going to deter Will from his fateful objective.

BLACKJACKS OF NEVADA

Ethan Flagg

Five years in prison have given Cheyenne Brady plenty of time to dwell on revenge after being left for dead during a hold-up by the Nevada Blackjacks. Upon his release Brady joins up with an old prospector, Sourdough Lamar; together they head for Winnemucca and the prospect of honest work. But when Brady's old gang, led by Big-Nose Rafe Culpepper, plans to rob the town's bank, Cheyenne is accused of masterminding the hold-up. Can he extricate himself from once again sinking into a life of crime?

INCIDENT AT FALL CREEK

D. M. HARRISON

As Charles Gilson's line of employment usually involves wanted dodgers and a sawn-off shotgun, when he receives news of an inheritance, he is determined to make a fresh start. But Gilson has competition for the money: Theodore Alden has charged his lawyer with securing it by fair means or foul. With everyone, including Town Marshal Hardy, against Gilson, the odds seemed stacked against him — it will take more than a few bullets to secure what is rightfully his . . .

WHITE WIND

C. J. Sommers

Spuds McCain is convinced the White Wind brings disaster to all those who sense its message. Hobie Lee is sceptical. But bad things do happen to the Starr-Diamond Ranch — Hobie is hoodwinked and ambushed into trouble when his charge, Ceci Starr, disappears on a trip to town. The White Wind blows away the rest of his common sense as he determines to restore the reluctant Ceci to her father: it will take a maelstrom of death and double-cross before it blows itself out and Hobie can find peace.